Milked

First Edition

Christopher Trevor

Milked

First Edition

Published by The Nazca Plains Corporation
Las Vegas, Nevada
2007

ISBN: 978-1-887895-66-8

Published by

The Nazca Plains Corporation ®
4640 Paradise Rd, Suite 141
Las Vegas NV 89109-8000

PUBLISHER'S NOTE
Milked is a work of fiction created wholly by *Christopher Trevor's*
imagination. All characters are fictional and any resemblance to
any persons living or deceased is purely by accident. No portion
of this book reflects any real person or events.

Cover, Greasetank
Art Director, Blake Stephens

Acknowledgements

To my Pedicure buddy Neil:
because you said I have beautiful feet...

Milked

Christopher Trevor

Contents

Introduction

Milked, milking a guy, or, as it is sometimes called, "Edging." I've known Christopher Trevor for some time now and when he told me about the subject matter of this latest book of erotic tales I nearly "milked" myself dry at the thought of it. An entire book of stories starring guys being milked repeatedly? Who else but Christopher would have thought of something like this? When Mr. Trevor approached me concerning this intro I was very flattered. Being a guy who loves tying up and tickling other guys I have found how "Cum Control" and "Surprise Milking" can really intensify a scene. Sometimes when dudes make tickle wagers they don't count on being milked. When they find that they are about to be repeatedly milked to the edge the scene takes on a whole new meaning. After a guy (or perhaps I should say "most guys") has shot his load his body tends to become hyper-sensitive to the touch, especially, as I have found in areas such as his slimy cum soaked cock and his nipples. So after that guy has cum please do help yourself to those areas of sensitivity. I guarantee he will be up and ready for another milking session very soon. Christopher said that "Surprise Milking" was a very apt way of stating it, given the stories that appear in this collection. Being a tickle fetishist I can honestly say that in between teasing a tied and tickled guy milking him slowly and repeatedly can be sadistically and erotically fun. I have a married buddy who when we get together that's all we do. I tie him up and as I tie him spread eagled on my queen-sized bed I tell him about the scene he and I will be acting out that night, wherein in between he will be slowly milked, repeatedly relieved of his ball juice so to speak. As I tell him the scene we will be enacting he is hard as concrete in the cock. I find that the anticipation mixed with a little fear really sets him in motion. He has a runner's build, nicely toned, muscular in the right places and a really thick cock, a cock meant for milking. Also, as I will get back to later in this intro I have found that the area behind his knees is very ticklish and sensitive. But it could take hours to really drain him as I love teasing him, denying him his orgasm till he's just about crazy with it; hence the need to keep him bound for the duration. To tie him I use a combination of ropes and cuffs of various styles. Usually he tries not to have sex with the wife for a few days before our secret meetings. In other words my married buddy agrees to our scenes but in the realm of the world of kink it is sadistically fun if he does not agree to it. It takes the scene to a more intense level. After a while of tickling him at what we call his pressure points and after a while of teasing his cock I milk him...*after* he shoots his load. That is the part that he loves/hates...and that is where the term "Edging" comes into play. Once a guy has shot that load, if you continue stroking him he is forced to dribble out those last drops of pearly seed. And as mentioned once a guy shoots his load he is real sensitive feeling. If you work him slowly enough after a while he will be erect again...and then you start it over. And it's at that point that most men in that position will want you to "Let go of it Dude, that's enough huh?" And as also mentioned he will be sensitive not just in the area of his cock. Find his sensitive spots and torment those as well after he's cum. He will love/hate you for it as you make him climb to new heights of ecstasy. As I stroke him after he's cum he respectfully asks that I stop. To keep the milking scene going I fiendishly ask him "Stop what?" As he writhes and struggles in his inescapable bondage I will tickle his legs behind his knees. I have found that that is one spot where he becomes ultra-sensitive feeling after having ejaculated. He is awfully ticklish there and as he giggles and squirms he manages to moan things like, "C'mon stop", trying at the same time to throw off my concentration. Instead of stopping though I continue tickling behind his knees and stroking his spent cock at the same time. Again I will ask him, "Stop what?" and he will helplessly reply, "Don't." To really make him batty I will dumbly respond "Don't what? What exactly is it you are trying to say?" Sputtering at that point and his cock helplessly hard again and aching he will then scream "C'mon Darryl, stop!! Okay, okay you win!!" He telling me "You win" is our "buzz" word. Sometimes just to be mean I'll keep stroking his slimy cock and ask him, "I win what buddy?" and then he will rant and rave like a captured marine as he again spurts a load for me, and there you have it, "Milking" or as it's also called, "Edging."

Seeing my married buddy struggle, watching him help-lessly shoot those loads gives me a feeling of total dominance and power, seeing that I can really control his agony/pleasure. In the end its all about control and my God, the look on his handsome face when I finally do untie him, he's usually red and sweaty, completely worn out...after all I have usually "milked" better than three loads from him in the time I keep him tied. Most times he will kneel on the bed just holding his head, rocking back and forth, catching his breath as it comes in small gasps. He whispers "Thank you" over and over and that feeling of power within takes me to new heights then. He is in his late thirties so a scene of this nature, being able to squeeze at least three loads from him could take upwards of a few hours, hence what I mentioned earlier, how he tries to refrain from having sex with the wife for a few days beforehand. A few times for our scenes I have made him swallow a Viagra tablet. Most guys do not need that enhancement but for the purposes of the stories that "Christopher Trevor" presents in this book Viagra can be meanly induced fun. And so, with all that in mind I thank my good buddy "Christopher Trevor" for seeking out my insights into one of my favorite pastimes...

-Darryl, the fiendish tickler-

A Boner Book

Milked Sailor

Name, Higgins, Rank, First class private seaman, Age, twenty two; Height, six feet two inches tall, give or take an inch here and there, weight, two hundred and ten pounds of solid muscle. Eyes, crystal blue, Hair, yellow blond, cut down to peach fuzz on my crew cut head. Situation, *code fucking red!!! Code fucking red Sir!! This sailor boy is in a shit load of trouble!!*

I had been on leave in upstate New York when this happened. Shit, nothing like this should happen to any military guy, let alone a sailor of my stature and good standing. Our ship had pulled into New York harbor and most of us had been granted a three-day pass to the city. I'm from down South where we like things pretty much quiet and serene, which was why I had decided to rent a car and spend some time up in the suburbs. No rough housing with my sailor buddies for me, no Sir, just some privacy and maybe a beautiful woman or two. I was driving my small rental car along a quiet road lined with trees and woods on both sides when the urge for a cold beer hit me like a ton of bricks. I figured one beer couldn't hurt, I would still be able to drive, no fucking problem Sir! But where oh where was a sailor boy going to get a beer on a lonely road like the one I was driving on? Chances were that I was going to have to wait till I got back to the bar in the lounge of the hotel, and that was still another twenty minutes of driving or so, maybe even a half hour. Then, as luck (Ha) would have it on the side of the road I saw a small building with a neon sign in the window that read "The Local Bar." Other neon signs in other windows of the place advertised Heineken, Coors, Budweiser and Amstel.

"Whoooo!!! Pay dirt Higgins ol' boy, pay fucking dirt, a real old fashioned watering hole it looks like," I whooped out loud, gripping the steering wheel tightly as I slowed down. "Get a nice cold one and maybe even meet some nice looking broad or broads and spend the night in their arms, takin' turns porkin' their rinds. YEE HAW!"

I was so glad (at that moment that is) that I had ventured out on my own. It looked to me like I had just found upstate New York's best kept secret Sir! The Local had a parking area in the back of it. I saw that there were numerous cars there so I figured the place had to be pretty lively. Hopefully it would be lively with women as well as drink. Fuck, *oh fuck,* thoughts of being stripped down to my socks and fucking some beautiful woman or two made my huge sausage-sized cock get hard and tent up in my white uniform trousers already. But *oh fuck,* little did I know at that moment just how much attention my big sausage was in for that night. Good Lord Sir, as I said, no sailor should suffer what I went through that night at the bar called "The Local."

"Easy big boy, easy," I said with a grin, looking down at my bulging and beefy crotch.

I parked my car, stepped out to stretch and gave myself a few moments for my hard-on to deflate for a bit. I would be stalked back up in no time mark my words on that. Dressed in my crisp white navy uniform complete with black patent leather lace-up shoes, a black neckerchief tied over my pullover white shirt (jumper) and a white sailor hat perched on my head I walked into the bar called "The Local."

The place was dimly lit; smoke filled and smelled of a mixture of alcohol, cigarettes smoke and sweat. I even detected a slight hinting aroma of marijuana in the air. Soft playing rock and roll music filled the stale air. On the right was a long bar with patrons seated on stools. Off to the side of the bar was a section of small tables. All the tables were occupied by patrons. On my left I saw a pool table. A few guys were engaged in what looked like a pretty intense game at that moment. I figured that after a beer I would join in on their next game. *(Right!)* The way the pool playing guys were looking at me I figured they would want me to play in the next round. *(Again, right!)* I mean, they were really looking at me Sir. Down a small hallway I saw a sign that read "Rest Rooms." Looking around some more I saw only men in the place. I had to wonder at that but I figured some women would show up soon. And, being the only uniform in the place I knew that I could score in a fucking heartbeat. Women were magnets for a tall handsome guy in a uniform after all. *(Right!)* I lit a cigarette and sat down on a vacant stool at the bar, wrapping my big feet around the rung at the bottom of said stool. The bartender, a rugged looking guy who looked to be in his late twenties, perhaps his early thirties, with brown hair, brown eyes and pretty muscular at about five feet ten inches tall was at my service in a microsecond.

"Good evening Sailor, what'll it be?" the bartender asked me politely.

"Cold, cold Budweiser my good man," I replied with a smile.

The bartender placed a bottle of brew in front of me along with a frosted mug. As he poured the beer into the mug I reached into my back pocket for my wallet.

"No, no Sailor, on the house," the bartender said to me. "Any military personnel that graces "The Local" drinks for free."

"Well thank you Sir, thank you very much, you are very kind," I said with a grin and took a pull on my cigarette.

I placed my cigarette in an ashtray and took a gulp of the icy cold beer.

"Ahhhhh, now that's good Sir, that is real fucking good," I said to the bartender and reached out to shake his hand. "Thank you again for the on the house special. I'm Private Higgins Sir."

He shook my hand and introduced himself as Jack.

"You on leave Higgins?" the bartender asked me, holding tight to my hand. "Vacation?"

"Yes Sir, three day leave actually, got to be back at the ship night after tomorrow," I said. "I came in here to have a cold one and hopefully meet me a hot one, if you know what I mean Jack."

"I think I do Private Higgins, *I think that I do at that,*" he said with a sly looking grin and finally let go of my hand. "And judging from what a handsome fucking guy you are you should have no problem tonight."

As I took another gulp of my beer Jack served a guy seated a few stools down from me. I looked around the place, giving it a good once over and still no women in the bar. Shit! When Jack was done serving the other customer I gestured to him. He came back over to me.

"Ready for another one already Private Higgins?" he asked me.

"No, no I'm just having one Jack," I replied. "I'm drivin'. Can't risk being pulled over for driving under the influence. I'm sure that some badass cop out there would just love to land my sailor boy ass in the clink for the night. Ha, God knows what he'd want to put me through huh? No way am I goin' to let that happen Jack. Listen man, where are the women in this place? All I see are men."

Jack smiled devilishly at me and nodded his head from side to side.

"Sailor Higgins, if women are what you're looking for tonight you are in the wrong place," Jack said to me, leaning toward me with his palms flat on the bar.

"Why is that?" I asked him, feeling totally confused.

"This is a man's bar," Jack said and winked at me. "If you know what I mean."

I sipped my beer and looked up at him in shock as he stood up straight.

"Y-you mean to tell me that I've gone and ventured into a fag bar?" I asked him in my Southern accent, placing my half-empty mug on the bar. *"Holy fucking shit, h-holy fucking shit..."*

"Hey, take it easy Sailor boy," Jack said to me. "You could still wind up getting lucky."

"Yeah? How?" I asked him angrily, mostly angry at myself for this twisted turn of events and took a pull on my cigarette. "I am not a fag Jack."

"Don't say that too loud in here Higgins, you are sort of

outnumbered, if you get my drift," Jack said. "But as I said, you could still get lucky."

"And I said, how?" I asked him through clenched teeth, thinking how all I wanted to do was bolt from the place yet my curiosity was piqued. "You going to have some women sent in here just for me? I mean, fuck man, here I am a horned up sailor boy sweating in my damned socks and I accidentally walk into a fag bar! And I'm a straight sailor boy Jack, straight with a capitol "S." So like I asked, you going to have some women sent in here for me?"

"Well no, but any one of these guys in here would just love to suck some hunky sailor boy cock I would bet." Jack said bluntly and wickedly, leaning close to me and taking the bottom of my neckerchief in his fingers and thumb. "I mean fuck, there would be no game playing, no small talk and no wining and dining to be done. Before you can even get near a woman's panties most times you have to buy her dinner, make small talk and even then that don't guarantee shit, unless you get yourself a hooker. And even then you would have to pay for it. In here, everyone knows what the fuck they're after Higgins. And let me tell you Sailor boy, almost every fucking guy in here is checking you out. I cannot believe they didn't mob you when you walked through the door."

Jeez, I must have been totally fucking oblivious not to have noticed these faggots on the prowl for me Sir. However, I sat there mulling over what Jack the bartender had just said to me as he continued to tug at my neckerchief.

"Just like that?" I asked him. "Some fucking queer is just going to suck my damned sausage?"

"Well, I'll tell you what," Jack said, leaning in still closer to me, his lips dangerously close to mine. "In the men's room here there's a stall with what's called a "glory hole" cut in it, right at crotch level. Judging from your height you would fit it just perfectly. *And*, the goddamned glory hole is cut in the front door of the stall, not on the sidewall like most other glory holes are. You head on in there stick your pride and joy through that glory hole and I guarantee the first guy that comes in there will have your sailor boy cock in his mouth in a heartbeat. Fuck man; just think about it as if it was a woman doing you. You'll be on the other side of the door as it is, you won't know from Adam who the fuck it is sucking your meat. A cock doesn't need to know who's sucking it for it to feel good Sailor Higgins."

Damn, the way the fucking guy was talking had me sweating some more in my socks that was for sure. Was I actually considering this?

"Holy fucks Jack, if I do this I get the distinct feeling that you want to be the one to get this horny sailor boy off," I said, my lips just about grazing his as he leaned in even closer to me, still holding me by my neckerchief.

"Not me you handsome fuck," he said with a grin. "I have to stay here and tend bar. You couldn't imagine what I would love to do to you though. No, I'm just giving you something to think about. And I will bet any fucking amount of money that your meat stick is harder than a diamond at the moment."

With that he gave me a fast peck on the lips, let go of my neckerchief and again stood up straight. Holy fuck man I had just been pecked on the lips by a guy. I sat there feeling very confused and *very, very fucking horny, sweating in my socks,* as I always say. I ran the top of my hand over my lips and moved my feet flat on the sides of the rungs of the stool. Jack took my sailor hat off my head, placed it on his head and ruffled my peach fuzz blond hair. I gulped down what was left of my beer, stubbed out my cigarette and stood up.

"Keep that hat warm Jack," I said with a grin on my face and a hard fucking boner of steel in my uniform pants. "I'll be back for it soon."

Jack gave me a thumbs-up and I walked away from the bar toward the men's room... I could feel eyes checking me out as I walked with my face forward, mouths were no doubt watering to get at my big sausage. I was making a nice impression in my uniform trousers after all Sir. I wondered which of the fags in this sleazy bar would be so lucky to get my stored up spunk. Ha!!

Fuck it all, I had been at sea for over four months and during that time I barely shot a load or two. Being cooped up on a ship with a hundred or so other guys doesn't give a poor sailor boy too much privacy Sir. I hadn't been able to jack off all that much so I sure had a goodly amount of my sticky juices to feed to some lucky queer tonight.

The men's room was medium sized with three stalls lined up against a wall and two urinals on the far wall. Across from the stalls was a small sink. The men's room was lit with three bare bulbs hanging from the ceiling and the scent of urine filled the air. Amazingly the floor was clean I noticed as I walked slowly over to the stalls, my black patent leather shoes making squishing sounds against the spotless tile. There was no one else in there at the moment. The stall with the "glory hole" carved into it was the center one. Smiling devilishly, I ran a couple of fingers over the sides of the hole. It looked like it wouldn't be big enough to stick *my* sausage through. Fuck, I'm a sailor with a cock the size of a marine's that is for fucking sure. Fucking A! I pulled the stall door open, stepped inside and closed and latched the door behind me. Standing there looking down at the glory hole I slowly unbuttoned the fly on my uniform pants, thirteen buttons to be exact. Not really believing what the fuck I was doing I shucked my pants and underpants down around my thighs and looked down at my huge pulsing nine inches of big fat man meat. Fuck man, my sausage was harder than fucking hard, sticking out all thick and stalked up, fully at attention from my blond pubic bush. All the months at sea were about to be relieved in one gulp when some faggot got his lucky ass in here I thought. I took my glorious sized manhood in hand and slid it slowly through the "glory hole" for all to see, along with my juicy plum sized balls. My cock and balls just made it through the hole. A chill went up my spine as I felt the shaft of my cock slide against the walls of the "glory hole." Fuck, but I am blessed and big, yes Sir, fucking A choice meat I have! I figured when I was soft after some joker fag had sucked me off it would be easier getting my pride and joy back in than it was getting them out there on display. I didn't know at the time but it would be more than a while before I saw my big cock and balls again. Outside the stall my cock stuck straight out long and hard, twitching a tad up and down, oozing droplets of pre cum. My balls hung low and rested chock filled against the outside of the stall door. I pressed the palms of my hands against the inside of the door and waited. I chuckled a few times at what a sight my cock and balls sticking out of that "glory hole" must have made. Ha, definitely not a picture for the family album Sir.

"Oh fuck, fucking fucks can't wait for some joker fag to get his ass in here and get my sausage in his warm mouth," I whispered to myself in my Southern accent. "Fuck, all I got to do is pretend its Pamela Anderson out there scoffing on my meat. Thanks Jack, glad I took you up on your advice."

A few moments went by and then I heard the door to the men's room open.

"Fuck man, did you see that hot lookin' sailor boy at the bar?" I heard a male voice asking. "Fucking guy was more hand-some than a movie star."

"You said it Alex, and, holy shit, lookit what I see man!!" a second voice said and then, looking downward I saw two pairs of feet, one clad in construction boots the other pair in sneakers, standing in front of the stall door.

Fuck, two guys, two fucking guys were about to suck me off. I would pretend one of them was Pamela Anderson and the other was Anna Nicole Smith, hardy, har, har Sir!

"Oh man Ronald, judging from those frosty white pants and those spit shined black military shoes I think it's your sailor boy in there," the guy named Alex said and I felt a hand jiggle my balls and then close on my stiff cock, making me shudder. "That you in there Sailor boy?"

I rapped an affirmative on the stall door.

"Looks like Sailor boy needs some help with this problem he's got sticking out here," Alex said, still holding onto my cock by the shaft as it pulsed with an energy all its own.

He cupped my sweaty balls in his hand and tugged on them as he held my throbbing rage hardness in his hand. I gasped softly and squeezed my eyes shut as the guy (thinking it was Pamela Anderson) handled me.

"Fuck Ronald, his cock feels like its alive in my hand, like its steel, fucking bone is pulsing like crazy," Alex said, holding my cock and tugging my balls some more. "These balls of his feel like he's got months of spunk stored in 'em."

I rolled my uniform shirt up over my nipples, leaving my neckerchief dangling around my neck and my dog tags visible. I pressed my big fleshy nips against the stall door and chills and thrills of delight and ecstasy coursed through my smooth muscular body. I always loved the feeling that emanated from my nips when they were pressed against something nice and smooth. I had no idea just how much trouble I was in at that moment, nor any idea of just how much time I would be spending in that damned stall that night.

"Hey Sailor boy, my name is Alex, my buddy out here with me is Ronald, we own this fucking dump," Alex said to me, my big hard cock still in his hand as he played with my balls. "We're sure gladder than glad you decided to come in here and give the place a little life and some class."

"I'm Private Higgins guys, *fuck,* I am sweatin' in my socks in here, think you two can cool a hot sailor boy down tonight?" I called out and then Alex squatted down and wrapped his warm wet lips around my big throbber. "Ohhhhhhhhhrrrrr, Ohhhhhhhh God, oh yeah, feels great, fucking A you guys, *fucking A!"*

Alex let go of my balls and he sucked me real nice. With my eyes closed I imagined it was Ms. Anderson. Visions of her huge tits swinging back and forth as she chowed on me went through my mind. Ronald squatted next to his buddy and went to work heartily licking and slurping at my big succulent balls.

"OHHHHHHRRRR yeah, fucking great idea Jack my man," I gurgled in ecstasy. "Fucking guys (Pamela and Nicole, yeah, that's it) are sucking my cock *and* lickin' my damned family jewels.

My big sausage pounded and throbbed in Alex's mouth as he ran his tongue and lips all over it, up and down the shaft, driving me crazy, making me sweat some more in my socks and sending me into a flight of ecstasy. It amazed me that he was able to get all of my huge girth into his greedy craw. Women I'd dated always complained how my cock was of the gargantuan size and were just too big for their mouth; oh fucking A am I blessed Sir!

"Damn, I'm fucking flying you guys," I said breathlessly. "Feels like I'm in the danged air force or somethin'."

"Sounds to me like we got a charming Southern boy in there tonight Alex," Ronald said and slurped his tongue snugly around one of my big testicles.

"UHHHHRRRRRR yeah, oh shit, that, that's fucking awesome," I grunted.

I didn't want to tell these two fags that no woman had ever worked my balls, didn't want them to know that I'd never experienced that before. But hoo man, the way that guy was sucking and slurping my testicle was magic. It seemed that women loved my cock but my balls were always too sweaty and mangy for them. Ha, sweaty and mangy balls huh ladies? Look at this shit now I thought meanly, got me a fag fucking polishing my randy smelly balls for me. The two men ran their hands up and down my legs and over my navy issued black patent leather shoes. Fucking fags were making me nuts sucking my cock and slurping at my stinky balls. I guess no matter how much a guy washes down there his balls area will always be randy and sweaty huh guys? I rubbed and rubbed my big pink nips against the stall door, making them hard and erect. Fuck all Sir but that felt good. I gave my sailor boy nips a hearty squeeze each and my sausage tingled madly in Alex's (Pamela's?) mouth. My fingers felt all leathery and rough as I teased my own nips.

"OHHHHHHHHH God you guys, I-I'm getting close already!! *Shit, I am going to cream like a son of bitch!!*" I grunted throatily.

I let go of my nipples, clenched my hands into fists and stood there riveted to the spot as I felt myself getting closer and closer to the fucking boiling point. Alex stopped sucking me,

Ronald stopped slurping my balls and the two men stood up straight outside the stall door.

"Okay Ronald, now," I heard Alex say and then he took my saliva soaked sausage in his hand.

He began stroking me and stroking me, his hand practically making love to my hardness. God but that felt sweet.

"OOOHHHHHHHH FUCK, yeah, stroke my slimy cock man!!" I gasped.

As Alex stroked me I suddenly felt a length of rope being wound snugly around my cock and balls.

"H-hey man, wh-what are you guys doin' out there?" I asked nervously and breathlessly, my eyes popping open. (Fucking Alex was stroking me in a way that I could barely speak.) "T-tyin' up my cock and balls? What's up with that shit? OHHHHHHHHH yeah, yeah, I-I'm getting there now you fucking guys!! Going to shoot a nice hot load of sailor boy spunk for you two! Fuck yeah, sweatin' in my socks as usual..."

There wasn't time to think about my cock and balls being tied up out there at the moment because it was just then that I shot a monster sized load of sperm for the two guys.

"OHHHHHHHHHRRRR yeah, fucking A and B this time you guys!!" I grunted madly in a sailor's passion as rope upon rope of thick creamy sailor boy soup erupted from my big sexy cock slit.

Globs of it landed all over the clean bathroom floor and the two guys whooped it up and cheered me on every time another mess of it erupted from me.

"Oh yeah Sailor boy, go for it, shoot that pent-up load," Alex said gleefully, still stroking and stroking me and stroking me some more.

I grunted and swore like a marine in passion as the fucking guy siphoned every possible drop of mess from my smelly balls.

When I was done Alex let go of my cock and I stayed hard as a fucking rock. My cock and balls tightly trussed out there now kept me that way and aching, fucking aching Sir at the same time.

"H-hey, *fuckers,* tied up my cock and balls!!" I ranted as they secured the length of rope around them, enough of it so that I couldn't get my pride and joy back into the stall. "Come on you guys, I can't get 'em back through the glory hole!!"

"That's just our plan Sailor boy," Alex chortled meanly and gave my cock a mean whirl and tugged on the short slack of the rope. "Do you think we're just going to let a hot looking sailor boy like you shoot one load and just walk the fuck out of here? No fucking way you handsome stud."

"WHAT the fuck man???" I swore. "What are you tellin' me here???"

"Every fucking cock hungry guy that comes in here tonight is going to have at this horse-sized cock and those juicy and stank balls of yours," Alex went on, sounding absolutely sinister. "How many loads do you think you can cook up for us Sailor boy?"

Alex gave my slimy and coated cock a few good strokes and then, believe it or not Sir I was off and shooting a second load.

"OHHHHHHHRRRR fuck, oh fucks, oh shit, got me fuck-ing creaming again you fuckers," I ranted angrily now. "Talented with those hands and mouths huh fuckers? Pl-please guys, oh shit, I'm all sensitive and real sexy down there after I've popped my load."

"That's what we're counting on Sailor boy, and away you go," Ronald said from above me as I went on spewing. "And fuck man, you're beyond sexy." As I shot globs upon globs of soupy sperm outside the stall Ronald had climbed up to the top of the stall. He pounced in, landing behind me.

"OHHHHHHH come on bud, let go of my damned cock out there, quit it already," I shouted when I was done creaming, but Alex continued stroking me, driving me nearly insane.

Fuck, I wasn't half as insane at that moment as I would be a while later, much later *and still in that stall...*

"Nice piece of ass you got here Sailor boy," Ronald said

and gave my smooth muscular melon shaped ass cheeks a squeeze each.

"Faggot, get your paws off me!!" I snarled angrily, turning my head just to look at the guy standing behind me. (Fuck, the way my poor cock and balls were tied off out there outside the stall door my head was the only thing I could safely turn at that moment.)

Ronald was a big husky muscular guy, a little shorter than I was though. He had dark hair, traces of a beard and mean looking eyes.

"*Fuckers,*" I said, sneering at him. "This is a rotten trick to have played on me. Tell your buddy out there to untie my damned cock and balls, *now!!*"

As I reached for the latch on the stall door Ronald gave my ass a really hard and loud slap.

"OWWWWWWRRRR!!" I roared angrily and the bastard slapped my ass again.

"Fucking shit head, *goddamned pervert!!*" I seethed and then from outside the stall Alex gave the short slack of the rope on my cock and balls a good hard tug. "UHHHHHHHHHHRRRR OH FUUUUUUCCCKKK..."

Alex yanking hard on my tied pride and joy had just the effect he wanted. I involuntarily slammed against the stall door, my arms splayed up at my sides. With my arms up like that Ronald quickly got my rolled up uniform shirt off me, pulling it in a fast motion over my head.

"H-hey, give me back my damned shirt!!" I yelled and watched miserably as Ronald tossed it out of the stall.

"Fuck, I was shirtless before I had even realized what the fuck had happened. And it was my own fault at that. Rolling up my shirt earlier to get at my nipples while I was being sucked off made it that much easier for the guy to snatch it off me.

"Catch Alex, and then get yourself in here, you have to see the smooth muscular body on this hunk of beef," Ronald said meanly.

I turned my head again to look at him, just as he grabbed

my wrists tightly and yanked them behind me. I stood there help-lessly and feeling real stupid with my damned uniform pants and my underpants around my thighs, my neckerchief and dog tags hanging around my neck.

"Oh man Sailor boy, are you in for a time of it in here tonight," Ronald said and slurped one of my earlobes, making me grimace. "Like my buddy said, every fucking cock hungry guy that comes in here tonight is going to have at that big meat pole of yours out there. And not to mention those big juicy balls of yours, but I will mention them what the hell? Oh fuck man, but the gods were smiling when they made you."

"Fuck man, if you let all those faggots at me I'll be milked dry before the night is over!" I ranted, trying to pull my wrists out of his grasp and grimacing miserably at the thought of guy after guy after guy sucking me the fuck off. "Good Lord in his heavens, but my cock and balls will be so sore and stinking of man spit! Those guys will suck me down to my piss you bastards!"

"And then some Sailor boy, milked dry as a bone and then some," Ronald said fiendishly and licked my ear.

"SLOB," I spat.

Just then Alex climbed into the stall and stood at my other side.

"*Holy fuck,* he's more than gorgeous Ronald," Alex said, pulling a length of rope from his pocket and tying my hands securely behind me.

"Ohhhhhhhhhh shit, no, *no, oh God no, don't fuckin' tie me up in here you faggots!*" I seethed. "Oh fucking fuck, what a night this turned out to be, captured by faggots, of all danged things!"

"You mean what a night it is going to turn out to be Sailor boy," Alex chortled.

Alex was a thin lanky guy with blond hair and blue eyes. He had a look on his face that seemed to personify mischief and a guy who wallows in playing dirty tricks on unsuspecting guys like me. After my hands were tightly bound behind me at the wrists the two men took delight and pleasure in running their mangy hands all over me. They reached around and in front of me and squeezed my big pink nipples, teasing the fuck out of them with their leathery rough feeling fingers and slapping my ass cheeks (hard) a few times each.

"OHHHHHHHHRRRR you fuckers, my poor nips are so danged sensitive and you two are squeezin' 'em like they were Charmin," I panted and my cock stayed rage hard outside the stall.

They squeezed and palmed my massive pecs, ran their hands over my peach fuzz blond hair and even kissed (fuck man, they kissed me) and slobbered over the back of my big navy man sized neck.

"Bastards, I swear I'll get you guys for this," I grumbled miserably.

"Man, this sailor is too hot for words Ronald," Alex said and slid my long black neckerchief off me. He wound it twice around my head and tied it over my eyes, effectively blindfolding me.

"Shit, shit, *shit,*" I grunted as I was plunged into total darkness.

Then, we heard the door to the men's room open and footsteps headed toward the stall I was now literally trapped in.

"Looks like you're about to have another customer at your font out there," Alex chuckled, hooking a claw-like hand around one of my muscular upper arms, his hand not quite making it all the way around.

Outside the stall whoever he was he squatted down and without ceremony slurped my manhood into his mouth.

"UUUUHHFFFFF…" I grunted breathlessly and leaned my forehead against the stall door as I was sucked toward blast number three.

"Fuck man, look at him suffering in ecstasy Ronald," Alex said as he and Ronald ran their paws all over me and the guy outside the stall feasted heartily on my cock, the sounds of slurping and swallowing filling the air.

"Mmm, nice big tasty cock you got out here buddy," the guy said and quickly gobbled me back into his greedy mouth and sucked.

"AAARRRRHHH," I grunted again and again in a mixture of ecstasy and exhaustion, wondering how something so humiliating as this could have befallen me. *"P-perverts!!"*

"We're perverts?" Alex asked me, jokingly tugging on the knot in my blindfold. "You're the guy who walked in here and stuck his cock through that "glory hole" for everyone to get at."

"I-I didn't plan it this way fucker," I seethed madly. "I-I didn't plan to be milked till my well was dry. I didn't plan to wind up tied the fuck up in here and blindfolded to boot. OHHHHHHHHH, fucking guy out there is goin' to have me spewing my damned sailor boy load all over again. Oh jeez man!!"

Alex and Ronald squeezed my ass cheeks real hard and twirled their fingers over and over my big nipples. Chills coursed through me, and goose bumps broke out all over me. Fuck it all, but I was being taken beyond the throes of ecstasy.

"OHHHHHHH fuck, oh yeah, fucking milking me, making me shoot my damned load," I panted as the guy outside the stall scoffed down my juices. "Fucking degenerate, swallowing my damned sailor spunk."

"If he's swallowing it there's no doubt in my mind that that's Eugene out there," Alex said to Ronald and the two men laughed meanly, still running their hands over and over me. "Fucking Eugene just loves drinking milk direct from the udder."

Eugene let my cock slip out of his mouth and it went semi soft, but I still wasn't able to pull it back into the stall, away from hungry mouths. What with the rope tied around it out there I wasn't going to be pulling my cock and balls back into the stall any time soon. And blindfolded with my hands tied there wasn't all that much I could do to help myself at all, oh fuck of fucks!"

"Sailor spunk huh?" Eugene called out to me, sounding delighted.

"Yeah man, I am a sailor in the USA navy," I called out angrily. "And you and these two other perverts in here are in deep fucking shit for what you're doing to me!! Hell, this is akin to kidnapping!"

"Two perverts?" Eugene asked. "That you and Ronald in there with him Alex?"

"Sure as shit Eugene, got the fucking hunk of a sailor boy tied up and blindfolded in here," Alex said, holding tightly to my upper arm, kneading my muscles. "Go on, he ain't going anywhere any time soon, help yourself to another batch of US navy soup, cooked up real fresh in Private Higgins's succulent balls here."

Before I could utter another word Eugene had my cock in his mouth again. He tugged meanly on my poor balls and really sucked me hard this time. Like I said, these guys would suck me down to my piss.

"AAAAYYYYYYRRR shhhhhiiiittt, you danged bastards!!" I fumed and then felt rope being wound around and around my biceps curls, around my upper body and then to the stall door.

"Climb out there and help me get him secured to the door Ronald," Alex said with authority in his voice. "I want this fucking hunky sailor boy *totally fucking immobilized.*"

"Fuckers," I whispered.

As Eugene sucked me toward another blast he pulled my uniform pants down around my ankles, revealing the tops of my calf length black nylon dress socks…

I grimaced miserably behind my blindfold and arched my head back, my teeth clenched in despair. As Eugene greedily chowed down on my big cock he toyed with the tops of my socks, snapping the elastic in them against my skin. There was something kinky yet wrong with that at the same time. When a guy is standing up straight no other guy should be able to be playing with his damned socks of all things! Alex and Ronald worked double time getting me roped tightly to the stall door. Man, was I in a fucking pickle or what!

"Fuckers untie me and let me the fuck out of here, *now!!*" I snarled dejectedly.

As if I had said nothing I was sucked, tied and groped more and more. When my upper body was tightly roped to the stall door Alex, still in the stall with me squatted behind me and pushed my sexy ass cheeks apart, revealing my pink gaping rosebud of a crevice.

"Hey, what are you doin' back there man?" I gurgled.

"Oh fuck, what a fucking piece of ass you got Sailor boy," Alex said lustfully and I could feel him staring wide-eyed at my twitching hole.

Then, he plunged his tongue deep into my opening.

"OHHHHHHHHHHHH ssshhhhiiitttt," I muttered, my lips trembling now. "Fucking butt muncher!!"

Outside the stall Ronald had joined Eugene at my crotch, slurping and sucking my starting to swell up balls as Eugene sucked my cock like a madman.

"Ohhhhhhrrrrrr," I seethed, knowing that any faggot in my position would have loved all this shit, as the three men feasted on me real heartily, like I was a buffet.

It took a while more than the first three times, but eventually I shot that fourth load. Fucking Eugene scoffed down my juices again, sucking the very bejesus out of my poor aching cock as he did so, wanting every drop of it as I came and came and came. Alex was dribbling furiously into my hole and sucking up his juices at the same time, sucking the walls of my shit chute. His tongue flicking around on the sides of my raunchy stink hole was making my head spin as I spewed my load down Eugene's throat.

"Ohhhhhhhhhrrrrr good lord, fucking bastards, perverts, got me creaming again!!" I ranted as my cock tingled numbly in Eugene's mouth.

"Holy shit, it seems like this hunky kid is a twenty-four hour beat off machine," Ronald marveled as I shot that fourth load of sperm.

But then, oh God then, I screamed anew in pain as Alex stood up behind me, brought his cock out of his jeans and slid it up into my saliva slicked shit chute.

"AAAYYYRRRRRR shit, *ohhhhhhhrrrrrr no, no, not this!!*" I ranted in pain as I felt Alex's cock slowly entering my most private crevice.

"What the fuck are you doing to him Alex?" Ronald asked from outside the stall. "Fucking the tar out of Sailor boy?"

"S-sure as shit Ronald my man, oh fucks, oh man, what a sweet piece of ass this kid has," Alex crooned, his hands squeezing my hips as he fucked me and fucked me. "His hole is just squeezing the fuck out of my cock every time I slide it up there."

"I'm going back out to the bar," Eugene said. "You two have fun now. Bye Sailor boy and thanks!"

"BASTARD!! LOWLIFE!!" I roared at Eugene as he left the men's room. "Ohhhhrrrrr shit, you sleazy scumbag, get your god-damned cock out of my hole man!!"

"Ronald, get yourself in here and sample this kid's butt hole," Alex called out breathlessly as he thrust in and out and in and out of my poor hole. Fuck man, I could plow this sailor all fucking night!"

I balled my tied hands into fists and leaned my head back in agony as I heard Ronald climbing back up and into the stall, the stall that had become my prison.

"Fuck, why'd I listen to that damned bartender?" I whimpered awfully.

"Oh God, I'm goin' to cum Ronald," Alex panted. "Fuck man, I am going to fill Sailor boy's hole with my juices! OH yeah, fuck yeah, OHHHHHHHH man!!!"

I felt Alex's warm, sticky load flood my hole as he grabbed my ass cheeks in firm tight grasps. Fucking guy kneaded my silky tight cheeks like crazy as he spewed and spewed his danged mess in me, using me like I was some cheap whore on a Saturday night.

"Fucking sick bastard, what the hell kind of shit is this?" I ranted as Alex's cock slid out of my hole. "Fuck a poor sailor boy up the ass and cum inside him as well like I was some kind of receptacle?"

But then, again, my words were cut short as Ronald took his turn at bat at fucking my hole.

"AAAAYYYRRRRR GAWD," I screamed in a man's pain as

Ronald's cock, bigger and fatter than Alex's invaded me next.

Ronald slammed his muscular body up against mine and buried his hugeness deep in my hole before he started thrusting in and out of me. His pillar of man meat felt like it was gargantuan as he speared me with it.

"OHHHHHHH yeah, you were so fucking right Alex, fucking great piece of ass he has, tighter than a drum and ass cheeks as smooth as silk," Ronald gasped and licked my earlobe.

"SLOB!!" I yelled again and felt Ronald's cock slide deep enough up inside me to touch my stinking shit.

When they were done they had each fucked me three times. A mess of sludgy cum and saliva dripped from my aching and twitching hole. Fucking bastards had also taken my uniform pants, my underpants and my shoes off me, leaving me clad in just my black socks, my dog tags around my neck and my neckerchief as a goddamned blindfold. They had tied my feet tightly together at the ankles as well, totally immobilizing me at this point.

"We'll leave his uniform and shoes outside the stall on the sink," Alex said as yet another bar patron sucked my cock now. "But I'm keeping his underpants as a souvenir of all this. I mean, how can you beat that huh? A sailor's underpants…God!!"

"Perverts, that's a shitty thing to do, lowest of the all time low, to steal a sailor boy's danged stinking underpants," I grunted as I was sucked off like crazy, the guy who had me in his mouth really applying pressure to my cock. "OHHHHHRRRRR SHIT Mister, easy with my cock huh?"

As the guy sucked me I felt fingers at my mouth and then as I stupidly parted my lips I felt a tiny pill wedged into my craw.

"H-huh?" I whimpered as the pill rested on my tongue and Alex or Ronald, I never knew who pressed my mouth closed.

"Nothing harmful Sailor boy, just a little something to help you along to shoot more potent loads while you're trussed up in here," Alex said.

I shook my head "No", not wanting to swallow whatever the fuck it was they were dosing me with. But then, a good solid punch to the ribs took care of all that.

"GGGGGRRRMMMFFFFF!!" I heaved and the pill slid down my throat.

"Wh-what'd you just feed me?" I asked angrily.

"Viagra, twenty milligrams Sailor boy, or should I say Sailor head?" Alex laughed and then I heard him and Ronald climbing out of the stall.

All the while the guy outside the stall went on and on sucking my meat pole. Viagra? Fuck, I didn't need no stinking Viagra to get my cock to rise to the occasion. As was coined earlier I'm a twenty-four hour beat off machine! I can get up and hard with a thought. But GAWD, now with a Viagra slithering through me and being sucked off by one guy after another I would be kept stiff and spewing all fucking night for sure Sir!

"When are we going to let him out of there?" Ronald asked Alex.

"Let's see, it's about eleven o'clock right now, I would say we should keep him in there till closing time, four AM," Alex chortled.

At those words I leaned my head helplessly against the stall door and literally stood there sweating in my damned socks. Never knew that that expression that I used so often would literally come true...

Cackling and laughing meanly Alex and Ronald wished me a good night and left the bathroom, leaving me alone with the patron who was presently squatting in front of the stall, sucking my damned cock.

"Mmmmm," the guy crooned, taking my manhood out of his mouth for a moment and holding it tightly in his hand. "Best piece of cock that's been sticking out of this stall in a long time."

I wondered if the last piece of cock that he was referring to had been tied up in there like I was. Shitty thing to have happened to a United States sailor let me tell you Sir. Fuck, if my captain could see me now I thought miserably. Holding my big sausage in his hand the guy outside the stall poked his tongue into my piss slit a few times and swirled the tip of it around in there, really getting me tingling. The way my cock stiffened all the more I could tell that the damned Viagra pill was working its magic on me.

"Arrrrrrrrrhhhhhhhh," I gasped as the guy's tongue drove my cock crazy.

"Likin' how that feels eh Sailor boy?" the guy asked me snidely. "Shit man, best idea anyone's come up with in a long fucking while, to tie a big cocked sailor boy up in this stall."

"It wasn't my idea that's for sure Mister!!" I blurted angrily.

Then, he wrapped his greedy lips once more around my throbbing boner and suckled it deep into his craw.

"UUUUUUHHH, damn you man, leave my poor cock alone already!!" I snapped breathlessly. "FUCK!!"

It took a long while, even with the Viagra doing its thing for me to shoot my danged load that time, but the guy didn't seem to mind in the least. He was truly enjoying himself sucking the fuck out of my cock and teasing my piss hole like crazy with the tip of his damned tongue. I supposed it had been a fantasy of his for some time to suck off a hunky slob of a sailor boy.

"AAAAAARRR GAWD, oh f-fuck man, cumming, I'm cumming *again!!*" I gasped a while later, sweat pouring off me everywhere at that point. "Shit, shit, never shot my load so much in such a short period of time!! OHHHHHHRRRRR jeez..."

He held my cock in his hand by the shaft, squeezed it tight and I shot small squirts of my juices this time. As I shot the last droplets of cum on the floor I heard the men's room door open and then close. The guy who had gotten me off was on his feet outside the stall at that point. My poor cock was still semi-hard, aching and dribbling small beads of piss and remnants of cum.

"Say, what the fuck is going on here?" I heard the guy who had just walked into the men's room ask.

The guy who had just gotten me off explained to the new guy that I was a hunk of a sailor boy and that the owners of "The Local" had tied me up in the stall for their enjoyment. Standing there in my socks I didn't utter a word as the two men talked about me. Before leaving the bathroom the guy who had last sucked me off gave my big sausage a fast squeeze and a jiggle.

"AAAYYYYYYYRRR SHIT," I gasped and he left the men's room, leaving me alone with whoever this new faggot was.

I squeezed my eyes shut under my blindfold and clenched my teeth in erotic misery as the new guy who had come into the men's room slurped my cock into his mouth…

Some sailor I had turned out to be. A lot of my shipmates told stories about all the women they scored with whenever we docked in some city. Some of them even told tales of scoring with two women at one time. They told of all the moist pussies and great blowjobs they would have to endure from women who simply adored handsome sailors. Of course I'd scored with my share of women as well Sir, but of all things, this time out I end up venturing into a sleazy gay bar, stripped to my damned socks, tied the fuck up in a bathroom stall of all places with my poor sausage-sized boner sticking out of a glory hole. Gawd, and with just about every faggot in the place having a grand old time with it. And not to mention the guys who loved feasting heartily at my low hanging nuts. God, my poor nuts felt like they were swollen to the size of tennis balls after a while. At one point two guys had squatted at the stall door but they didn't suck my cock. No Sir, all they wanted was some sweet and juicy sailor boy balls. Those fuckers each gobbled one of my testicles into their mouth and sucked and slurped 'em like they were the last source of nourishment on God's green earth. I thought for sure the way they were suckling my nuts that they were going to chew them right the fuck out of my sac. DANG!! Even if I did somehow manage to get myself and my cock and balls untied I wondered how the fuck I would get them back through that glory hole. The way my poor nuts had swelled up in my sexy sweaty sac that would be no easy task Sir let me tell you. Fuck, fuck, *fuck*… Standing there the way I was I probably could have struggled and used all my musculature to simply tear the stall door off its hinges. But then, if I did that I ran the risk of the unhinged door falling forward and taking my privates with it, hence, that would really put me in an awful set of circumstances. I could just imagine paramedics called in and seeing a sailor boy tied up to a stall door on the floor in a bathroom of a sleazy fag bar.

A couple of hours later I was *still* in that damned stall and feeling pretty much wasted and used up to tell the truth. I was still tied and blindfolded, sweating in my socks as two guys outside the stall were taking turns sucking my marine-sized cock while another guy who had climbed into the stall was licking, slurping and lapping feverishly at my grunge and cum soaked asshole.

"OHHHHHHHHHHHH fuckers," I groaned breathlessly and miserably, my sweat sopped forehead leaning against the stall door. "Bastards, why won't someone untie me?"

"Bet you're feeling real good huh Sailor boy?" the guy eating my hole said up to me, holding my ass cheeks apart and squeezing them hard. "The way I hear it you've been in here for quite a while tonight."

He gave my hole a good hard suck and squeezed my cheeks harder yet.

"And from what I also hear out at the bar you're going to be here a while more to come, and come, and come, and come," the guy taunted me and pursed his lips against my gaping and pink hole.

He toyed with my black socks as he slurped my damned stink hole. I had lost count at that point of how many times I had shot my load. Even the damned Viagra pill that had helped me along seemed to have worn off and I found myself really working to shoot my load after a while, while being sucked off. I had lost count of how many guys had eaten and fucked my hole. I just knew that I was just about going crazy with it all by then. My cock was sore beyond reason and when the two guys outside the stall got me off I shot just a very small spurt of sailor boy goop.

"OOOHHHRRRRRRR jeez Louise, fucking perverts," I grunted throatily as I came for what felt like the umpteenth time that night.

As I shot my small squirt the guy in the stall stood up and slid his hard cock into my very saturated hole.

"OHHHHHHH no, no, *no,*" I pleaded as his big cock invaded me.

He moved his huge hands over my bowling ball sized biceps, kissed the back of my neck and thrust hard and deep inside me, banging his cock against the deep innards of my hole.

"OHHHHHHHH yeah Sailor boy, it feels real good in there," the guy panted. "Fucking hot sailor, you got a nice tight squishy hole. Didn't think I was going to leave without sampling this hole of yours did you?"

He fucked me for a good ten minutes or so, not once stopping for air. He filled my hole with his donation of spunk and then he and his two buddies who had been outside the stall left the men's room, laughing meanly.

"Ha, ha, can you imagine what his buddies would think if they saw him now?" I heard the guy who had fucked me say laughingly.

"Fuck yeah, too bad there ain't two more sailors tied up in the other two stalls," one of the guy's who'd sucked me added. "I would cut "glory holes" in those stall doors myself for that..."

"Shit, my buddies," I whispered and cried large tears behind my blindfold.

It was a few minutes later when I heard the men's room door open again. I shuddered in fear knowing that my poor cock was about to endure more nastiness. When I heard whoever was in the bathroom climb into the stall behind me I shuddered even more, knowing that they were planning on porking me in the ass. Suddenly, my sailor hat was placed on my head.

"Didn't I tell you that you would have a great time in here Sailor Higgins?" I heard a familiar voice ask me.

"J-Jack?" I asked desperately. "Is, is that you man?"

"Sure thing, your favorite bartender," he said and gave one of my ass cheeks a hard squeeze. "So, what do you think? Got your rocks off more than you expected to tonight huh?"

"J-Jack, get me out of here man, shit, I feel like every fucking guy in this place has had at my cock," I stammered madly, grimacing miserably, sweating profusely by then. "I-I don't think I can stand it anymore. I'm feeling crazy here man. Fucking owners of this place got the drop on me and stripped me to my socks, tied me the fuck up real tight like this and fucking blindfolded me too man! I've been just about milked dry and my poor sausage and nuts are aching like I cannot fucking believe!"

"Yeah, Alex and Ronald can be practical jokers, that is for sure," Jack said, tugging at the mounds of rope tied over and over my upper torso and around the stall door. "They sure got you tied better than tight, that's for sure. Not to mention that you smell all randy and sexy in here."

He took a deep breath and inhaled my randy and sexy scent.

"Come on Jack, untie me man, *I have to get out of here, I cannot stand it anymore,*" I panted and heard the men's room door open and footsteps approaching the stall. "Oh fuck man, too late Jack, there's another dude in here and...OOOOOOHHHHHH shit, *fucker has my cock in his mouth already!! Didn't even bother to say hi...*"

As I was sucked upon heartily again Jack stood there running his mangy hands over my muscular sweaty body.

"Are you thirsty Higgins?" Jack asked me and put a bottle of cold beer to my trembling lips.

And so, as I was sucked again Jack fed me a cold Budweiser. I hadn't planned on a second brew that night, seeing as I was driving, but at the moment I needed it Sir. I was thirsty as all hell. I gulped the beer down gratefully between gasps as my poor sore cock was sucked hard. Some of the beer dribbled out of my mouth and Jack thought it was real sexy as it dripped down my chest from my chin.

"That's it Sailor boy, down the hatch," Jack said, forcing me to guzzle the beer as he rubbed his crotch against my ass.

I didn't even notice it as he sneakily stuck a tiny Viagra pill in the side of my mouth as I sipped and sipped the beer. It was as the pill went down my throat that I noticed it having been placed in my mouth.

"RHOOOOO no," I gurgled as Jack fed me the last of the beer.

"Getting me all gassed and pumped up again eh you fuck-er?" I garbled as Jack pressed his steely feeling crotch against my backside.

"Good God almighty, what I said to you back at the bar, about you not imagining what I would want to do to you in here…" Jack whispered in my ear. "Hate to do it to you Sailor boy, seeing as we became friends here and all, I realize you're straight too, but *I am* going to fuck the tar out of you."

He fed me the last drops of the beer and my head was spinning and my cock was tingling already from the new dose of Viagra I had been tricked into swallowing. My cock went numb in the guy's mouth outside the stall. As my cock was being used like a sex toy I heard Jack pull the zipper down on his pants and he slid his big tool deep inside me. Fuck, I felt like I was being speared in two by the horny bartender.

"OHHHHRRRRRR GOD, oh no, not you too Jack," I gasped miserably, choking on my tears.

The fucking guy felt like he had a monster-sized cock as he held onto my big biceps and thrust rudely and meanly in and out of my poor hole.

"God almighty, your muscles are like iron Sailor boy," Jack panted, his cock sliding in and out of me. "Sure glad you're tied up like you are, *and blindfolded.*"

He squeezed my biceps real hard, fucked me like crazy and the guy outside the stall was slowly bringing me toward yet *another climax* as the Viagra Jack had fed me took effect. My cock tingled madly in the guy's greedy mouth as he sucked me and sucked me and sucked me and sucked me some more. I don't think anyone cared anymore if I shot a load or not at that point. They were just having too much fun sucking my big sailor cock and fucking the tar out of me over and over.

"OHHHHRRRRRRR GOD, *what a fucked up night this turned out to be!!*" I garbled throatily and felt myself getting close to shooting my load again.

Jack went on and on fucking my hole…

A while later I had shot my small squirt into the guy's mouth outside the stall. After Jack had spewed his big creamy load into my hole I was alone in the men's room. I figured that it must be slowing down out at the bar because it seemed pretty quiet as I stood there in my socks panting and sweating like a pig.

"By all that's holy and by my military oath I swear that I will make the owners of this place pay for this shit," I whimpered miserably.

But how??? Was I going to go to the police and report this? I would be the laughing stock sailor boy of the world. Fuck, in a way I had put myself in this blasted situation. I wiggled my toes in my socks and stood there on my poor tired and aching feet. God almighty, but how many hours had gone by at that point? But then, as luck would suddenly have it in my favor, as sweat dripped over my tied wrists I felt the ropes unexpectedly move down closer to my hands. The moistness of my sweat had caused the ropes to slide down I supposed. Also, I think that the way I kept flexing the huge muscles in my arms and forearms must have caused the ropes to loosen slightly and slide down. Well, whatever the fuck had caused the ropes to move closer to my hands and loosen, it didn't really matter now did it Sir? *But could I get myself untied?* That was the sixty-four thousand-dollar question Sir. Saying a silent prayer I wiggled my long fingers toward the ropes around my wrists and felt scrupulously for the knots. I found a knot and began toying with it with the tips of my shaking fingers, sweating more and more. As I did so I heard the door to the men's room open and then close. Shit!! I worked faster poking and rubbing the knots in the ropes, loosening them.

"Oh man, I got to fucking piss," I heard a drunken sounding voice say outside the stall.

Obviouly he hadn't noticed my cock and balls sticking out of the glory hole. As I rubbed the tips of my fingers over the knot I had found I heard the sounds of pissing in the stall next to the one I was (trapped) in. I had to work faster if I was going to get my hands untied. As I did just that, loosening the knot, I wondered miserably how the fuck I would get my poor cock and balls untied after I was untied in the stall. After about twenty seconds or so the sounds of pissing stopped and the guy breathed a loud sigh of relief. I heard the stall door next to mine open and then the guy was washing his hands.

"Holy shit, some sailor boy left his uniform and shoes in here," I heard the drunken guy say stupidly.

Obviously he had found my clothes on top of the sink where those fuckers Alex and Ronald had left them earlier. God, it seemed like so long ago at that point that they'd captured me and stripped me down to my danged socks.

"Hmmm, Sailor boy must have really big feet," the guy said. "Fucking smelly feet at that too."

I grimaced under my blindfold in disgust when I realized that the guy must have been sniffing the insides of my damned shoes. I finally managed to get the tip of one finger under one of the knots. I held it there and took a deep breath.

"Holy fucking shit, it looks like Sailor boy is still here," I heard the guy outside the stall say drunkenly and in shock. "That you in there Sailor boy? "Y-yes it is, yes Sir, it is," I replied softly, my finger still under the knot in the ropes.

"Holy fucking shit again, how did you wind up in a situation like this?" the guy asked me and took my cock by the tip with his thumb and first two fingers.

I gasped loudly as he held my sore and aching cock straight out. With my teeth clenched I pushed my finger up against the knot I had found. It came loose.

"Oh yes, oh yes, thank you God," I whispered.

But my ordeal was still far from over. As I slowly got the ropes off my wrists the guy began stroking my slimy sausage, very roughly.

"AAAARRRRGGGGHHHH gawd," I heaved madly. "Hey man, that's my cock out there, not some goddamned play toy."

"Yeah, you going to stop me from doing what I want with it Sailor boy" he asked me mockingly. "The way you're all roped up like a caught steer I doubt it."

As he stroked me meanly my poor aching balls crashed against the stall door, sending blinding pain through me at what felt like a hundred miles per hour.

"OHHHHRRRRR *shit,*" I gurgled. "God almighty you fucker, let go of my cock out there!!!"

The ropes fell from my wrists. That done I was able to move my hands out to my sides, thus loosening the ropes around my upper body and the stall door. The guy stroked me harder and harder. Then, searing pain coursed through my very being as he held my cock in the palm of one of his hands and whapped it hard with what I guessed was one of my shoes.

"AAAAAYRRRRRRRR!!! Ohhhhhrrrrrrrrr *you sick fuck!!!*" I roared.

"Just proving my point Sailor boy," the guy chuckled.

As I got the ropes around my upper body untied the guy stroked my poor hurt cock. He obviously didn't see the ropes falling away from the stall door. After what he'd just done he should know that once out of there I would surely pound his ass into the pavement.

"OHHHHHRRR fuck, going to make me fucking cum man," I gasped as the Viagra did its work and I reached up with a trembling hand to pull the blindfold down from my eyes, leaving it dangling around my big neck.

As my eyes adjusted back to the light (fuck man, I had been blindfolded for hours) I shot another small squirt.

"OHHHHHHRRR GODS," I moaned, arched my body back and pressed my palms against the stall door.

The fucking guy whapped my poor cock again with one of my shoes as I came.

"AAAYYYYRRRRRR!!! You sick faggot!!" I grunted as he kneaded my softening cock in his hand, treating it real badly.

When I was done shooting my small squirt in his hand the guy put my shoe down, let go of my cock and exited the men's room. Jeez, I didn't even hear him wash my mess off his hand.

"Fucker," I whispered angrily, huffing for breath.

I unlatched the stall door, stood up on my toes and slowly,

so slowly opened it, moving vigilantly backward on my tied-socked feet. I looked like some sad excuse for a ballet dancer up on my toes like that. Shit, if I lost my balance I could very well say good-bye to my pride and joy. Up on my toes was no easy chore let me tell you. I managed to reach around the stall door and on the first try I grasped the slack of the rope around my cock and balls. I jiggled the rope around and around and finally they were free, *my cock and balls were free.* I pulled them gratefully but slowly back into the stall. Looking down I grinned from ear to ear at the sight of my huge sausage and saliva soaked swollen nuts.

"Good to see you again guys," I chuckled, realizing how silly it must have looked to be standing there in just my socks and talking to my cock and balls. "Bet you're feeling real tired."

I squatted down and untied my socked feet, pulling my socks back up to my calves as well. Finally free, I swung the stall door all the way opened and stumbled out.

"UUUHHHRRRRR GODS, fucking bastards," I grunted and leaning over grabbed the side of one of the sinks.

My hat slid off my head. I caught it and placed it on the stack of my clothes on the sink next to the one I was clinging to. I thanked God that none of the patrons decided to steal my uniform. I stood there catching my breath, my cock and balls tingling madly, my muscular body sopped and glistening with sweat and my poor head spinning like crazy. What a sight I must have made standing there in just my damned socks. Droplets of cum and saliva dripped liberally from my asshole and landed on the floor at my feet behind me, humiliating!!!

"God, God, *fuckers drove me batty in there,"* I whimpered, turning my head and looking at the stall I had been in all that time, practically all night from my best guess. "Bastards even fucked my ass, *shit, shit!!!"*

Standing there in my socks and sweating rivers I turned on the cold water in the sink. I gasped over and over and threw handfuls of cold water on my face. I cupped my hands together in front of me and filled them with cold water, gulping it down over and over, slaking my overpowering thirst. My poor cock was hard and tingling ala the Viagra I supposed. I stood up straight, took a hearty breath and grabbed it in hand.

"oooooohhhhh shit, fucking guys got me more worked up than a marine at wartime," I snarled loudly, stroking my aching cock over one of the sinks, my low hanging balls swinging real sexily. "uuuuuuuuuhhhhhhhh!!!!"

As I said I must have made a pretty sexy picture standing there like that, jacking off like a madman, wearing just my damned socks, naked as the day I was born, my muscular sweaty body arched back. And now, fuck; now I was stroking my own big sausage-sized meat stick. It took me a while Sir, but unbelievably I came again, the very small squirt of my sailor boy jizz landing in the sink.

"Fucking perverts in this place, *going to make them pay that is for sure Sir,*" I whispered angrily and still holding my cock in hand pissed into the sink I had just cum in. "AAAAAHHHHHH, shhhhiiiiiittt, never felt so damned good to piss."

When I was done pissing, and pissing, and pissing my poor cock finally went soft. It looked a little purple in spots from the whaps the guy had given it with my damned shoe, but I was sure it would be okay. I'm a tough cocked guy after all, hardy har, har Sir. My hole was more than hurting from having been fucked so many times and I wondered how long it would be before that would be okay. From the way it felt I also wondered how long it would be before I didn't dread having to take a dump. Standing there I felt my hole twitching and itching as more droplets of sludge and spit dripped from it. I shuddered. I was about to grab my uniform pants and begin dressing when the men's room door opened.

"I just want to see how that sailor boy is doin' in here," Alex was saying to Ronald as the two men entered the men's room.

At the sight of me standing there in just my socks, my dog tags and my neckerchief around my neck their mouths dropped open in surprise and hunger. Good God in his heavens, but the way they were looking at me it was as if they were prepared to eat me alive.

"Holy fuck, how'd you get out of there Sailor boy?" Alex asked me, pointing at the stall with the glory hole carved in it. "Fucking guy man, you managed to get yourself untied somehow!"

"Never mind that you perverts," I seethed through clenched teeth, dropped my uniform pants back on the sink and raised my big hands into fists. "Fuck man, I was milked practically dry in that damned stall!! And you bastards fed me Viagra, of all things, you jokers drugged me and made me all sexy for those faggots that found their way to me! Well, I'm not tied up now fuckers so I'm prepared to teach both of you a much needed lesson in respecting military guys like me!"

As the two men approached me I stepped forward as well, my hands clenched tight into big meaty fists. But as I threw out my first and only punch as I stepped forward some more one of my socked feet slid into the puddle of my cum from earlier. Being that I was totally winded and slightly buzzed *(and lets face it in a lot of throbbing pain in my most private areas)* Alex and Ronald dodged me as I went slip sliding in my own juices. I bucked and wobbled stupidly on my socked feet and as I did so Ronald, that big husky bruiser managed to grab my flailing arms and yank them behind me.

"AAAARRRRRHHHH, c-c'mon you bastards!!" I grunted, swinging my socked feet out as Ronald gripped my upper arms tighter and hoisted me up to my toes.

"Fuck man, you're sweating and stinking like a stuck pig Sailor boy," Alex quipped and ran a hand over my sweat sopped chest.

At his touch my semi hard cock twitched between my legs.

"Tell your fucking friend here to let go of me and then we'll see just how anxious you two are to have at me," I rasped angrily and in response Alex curled a hand around my slimy cock. "OHHHHRRRRR GAWD, I-let go of my sausage you freak!! OHHHHHH SHIT!!!!"

As Alex stroked me Ronald hoisted me up and down on my socked feet, playing rock a bye with me. My head spun into a reverse orbit and I was sweating more and more.

"OHHHHHHHHH you fuckers, blasted freaks, making me seething and crazy now!!" I grunted miserably.

"Good Lord Sailor boy, you really are in a lather huh?" Alex quipped as he stroked me up unbelievably to a new and painful, tingling hard-on. "You're more over sexed than a nymph in heat." Then, Ronald held me aloft as I had a breathtaking orgasm, but I only felt a tingling sensation in my numbed cock as Alex stroked a painful climax out of me.

"AAAYYYYRRRRR fuckers got me shootin' dry fucking loads at this point!" I panted miserably. *"Shit man, holy fucks, that can really make a poor guy go insane!! OHHHHHHHH SHIT…"*

"Looks to me like there's no more semen in this seaman," Alex quipped and the two men laughed meanly and hysterically.

I guessed that the Viagra had worn off at that point…

"OHHHHHRRRRR man, you degenerate, I-let go of my cock already," I gurgled.

When I was done and feeling totally wasted Ronald lowered me to my feet and Alex took my underpants out of his back pocket. As Ronald continued to hold me in his tight grasp Alex wiped the sweat from my body with my briefs, actually his briefs now that he had confiscated them from me, GAWD!

"OHHHHHH man, never mind wipin' me down," I whimpered, my cock hanging soft and shriveled between my muscular legs. "J-just let me get dressed and get the fuck out of here. You and your buddies out there have had more than enough fun with this sailor boy for one night!!"

"Get the fuck out of here?" Alex asked me in surprise, tucking my stolen underpants back into his back pocket and taking my neckerchief off my neck. (My heart thundered in total fear.) "Sailor boy, it's still a couple of hours till closing time. We're putting your sexy ass back in that stall, *now!!*"

With that Alex blindfolded me again and I struggled madly as Ronald and he both held me by one arm each as they moved me toward the stall.

"NO, no, *oh fuck no, c'mon you guys,*" I grunted as I bucked and struggled in their grasps, kicking my legs out as they moved me along.

"And this time we're going to tie you even tighter in there Sailor boy," Ronald said wittily, holding tight to my arm as he and Alex pushed me along on my socked feet.

I felt their knees pressing against my rear end at one point as they both pulled my muscular arms behind me and prodded me on.

"OHHHHHHHRRRR GOD NO, no, not this again you scum bags!!" I ranted madly to no avail. "Aw, c'mon you guys..."

They hoisted me up off my feet, slammed me against a wall and then stunned, there was no more struggling as I was brought into the stall...

In what seemed like no time I was again tied in the stall with my poor cock and balls sticking out of the "glory hole." Ronald hadn't been kidding earlier. This time I was tied so fucking tight that I could not move an inch of my body. They had even pressed my fingers flatly together and roped them up tight as well, preventing me from getting to the knots in the ropes around my wrists. It was Alex who had figured out how I had gotten myself untied. I stood there sweating in my socks all over again and whimpering as two new guys helped themselves to my now very smelly and over-cooked sausage and my family jewels...

Each time I shot a dry load (and it was a lot of times let me tell you Sir) I thought I would lose my mind for sure. I have no idea how many more guys had at my cock that night, but it was quite a few that was for sure. I also wondered how many of them had come back for seconds or more. I mean, lets face it Sir, its not everyday I'm sure that a hunky sailor boy is tied up in a stall with his pride and joy sticking out of a "glory hole" in the men's room at "The Local." No one climbed up into the stall to fuck me anymore but overall every time that men's room door opened and my cock was sucked I cried big tears behind my blindfold...

At four AM the bar closed. At ten after four Ronald came in

the men's room to finally untie me. I was feeling too beat to shit and too fucking weak to even think about trying to do anything as I stood there outside the stall totally naked now. Fucking Ronald had taken my damned stinking socks off my feet and tucked them halfway into the back pocket of his pants as a souvenir. Fucking perverts, they stole my under shorts and my damned stinking socks as well! With my hands trembling I began getting dressed…

When I was clad in my uniform it felt sort of strange not having my socks and underpants on, but I wasn't worried about that, no Sir! My goal was to get out of that place and be on my way, get out of there before they decided to get me roped up in that stall yet again. I kicked the stall door angrily and headed toward the door to the men's room. I emerged slowly from the men's room. As I walked down the short hallway my cock and balls aching in my uniform pants I saw Alex and Ronald sitting at the bar, both of them sipping beers. Jack was behind the bar. My underpants and socks were on the bar in front of the two practical jokers. A strange feeling of loss seared through me seeing my socks and underpants on the bar and not on me where they rightfully should be.

"Fuckers," I whispered angrily at them and felt goop seeping again out of my hole, staining the back of my uniform pants.

"Have a good night Sailor boy," Alex said to me, not turning around to look at me though. "Hope you really enjoyed yourself here at "The Local."

"Yeah, you come back real soon now you hear?" Ronald asked me snidely, picked up my black socks and sniffed them. "There's always a place for you here whenever your ship is docked."

"Mother fuckers," I seethed and left the bar.

At four thirty AM a tired and beat to shit looking sailor boy left the bar called "The Local" and walked slowly to his car in the parking lot, minus his socks and underpants….

I stood next to my car with my hands resting on top of it. I was gasping, heaving and crying. When I finally got myself under control I took my car keys out of my pocket, opened the door and sat down behind the wheel. It would be days before I shot another liquid load I thought miserably. Fucking faggots had milked me drier than dry.

As I thought about what I had gone through tied up in that stall my cock grew surprisingly hard and tented the front of my uniform pants. I climbed out of the car and coming out of the bar and quickly over to me I saw Alex and Ronald.

"You boys don't waste any time do you?" I asked them, my heart pounding in what felt to be overdrive as they came over to me.

Smiling wickedly the two men scooped me up off the ground and slung me across their shoulders…

"Fuckers," I garbled as they lugged me back into "The Local."

Alex and Ronald had me stripped and tied up again in that stall in what seemed like no time whatsoever. With my cock and balls sticking out of the glory hole Alex, Ronald and even Jack the bartender took turns sucking and slurping my aching cock and balls. I stood there sweating, *but not in my socks this time.*

A Boner Book

Neil the Sheer Socked Detective and the Fiasco in the Locker room

"OHHHHHHHHH GOD, you fuckers, you bastards, *you miserable lowlife scumbags!!!*" I ranted madly at Mr. Wilkinson, the man I had been hired to shadow, hired by his wife no less to prove he was cheating on her.

His two well-muscled buddies held me restrained by my upper muscular arms, me hoisted a few inches off the floor as Wilkinson held me by my exposed cock in the locker room of the gym that I workout at on a regular basis. How humiliating is that I ask you, to be being held by the cock by the husband of your client? GOD!!! And to add to my humiliation my cock was rock hard in the son of a bitch's hand as he held me good and tight, fear hard is what I would call it, no way I would get excited from being captured with my pants down (or off) so to speak. Right? Yeah, right...

"Y-you can't do this to me Wilkinson!!! I'm a detective, a private detective, UHHHHHH!!!" I grunted as my sheer socked feet dangled scant inches above the floor as the pervert slowly stroked my fear hard cock, my hairy balls hanging real low as he worked me. "Fuck it all man, OHHHHHHHHH, GOD, *let go of my cock you degenerate!!*"

I struggled mightily but to no avail in the two muscle monster's grasps, seeing as I was totally winded and exhausted from the workout I had just punished myself through. Wilkinson, smiling wickedly stroked my pulsing manhood a tad faster, really increasing the tempo as he worked me. I was sweating in my sheer socks, feeling myself getting close to that impending gusher. God and how mortifying would that be I ask you, guy to guy of course? Fuck, *fuck*, this twisted turn of events had been totally unexpected. Needless to say it was shocking for a detective of my caliber and stature, the hunter being captured by the game so to speak. And captured in just my garters and sheer socks no less, with everything I had on total display for the pervert and his two mean muscle cronies to play with.

"Well, needless to say and quite the contrary Detective, my buddies and I *are* doing it to you," the philandering husband said with a grin as he stroked me faster yet, pressing my white sweaty and stinky briefs against my nose and mouth with his other hand. "And we're going to do lots more to you before we're done here tonight. This little experience will teach you to meddle in other people's business."

My cock was by then better than rock hard in his hand I'm embarrassed to say, all eight or so inches of it…as my huge kiwi sized nuts hung and swayed in the wind.

"F-fucker, get those rancid under shorts away from my face," I seethed.

"What's the matter Detective?" Wilkinson asked me snidely, stroking and jiggling my cock now as my balls bounced back and forth under my raunchy ass crack. "Is the smell of your own manhood getting you close? Fuck, you shouldn't have been shadowing me Detective. Just look at the trouble your work has gotten you into now."

"N-not half the trouble you're going to be in when I report this shit to the police you philandering bastard!!" I ranted at him as his two muscle buddies held me tighter, snickering at my sides, my muscular hairy chest jutting forward as they yanked my arms behind me. "I'm a New York detective Wilkinson, I have friends in high places, and what you're doing here is illegal!! For the record you and your two goons have kidnapped me and you're fucking raping me man!! OHHHHHHHHH f-fuck!!"

Wilkinson simply smiled again and helped himself to a sniff or two of my randy underpants.

"PERVERT!" I grunted at him, trying desperately to disengage myself from his two muscular cronies' grasps and his and get to my locker where my handgun was in the side pocket of my suit jacket. "Sniffing my damned under shorts, my God Wilkinson, your wife was right when she hired me to prove you were cheating on her! *You really are a slob!!*"

But then, at that point there was no holding it back anymore. As the sleazy guy stroked my big cock I felt it.

"OHHHHHHHH FUCK, you goddamned pervert," I seethed and thick globs of my man juices erupted from my wide sexy cock slit as I was forcibly milked. "AAAAARRRHHH yeah, got me creaming my load like a bitch in heat, f-fuck, sweatin' in my socks like crazy here!!"

"Ha, ha, ha, ha, ha, ha, ha, ha, ha, ha, that's it Detective," Wilkinson laughed and so did his buddies as I flopped around in their grasps, my cum chugging out of my cock. "Ha, shoot that load for me bud. Show me how much you love me, ha! Fuck man, if my wife could see you now!! HA, her detective captured, wearing just his prissy sheer socks and shooting a load the likes of which I'm sure you haven't shot in a long while, ha!! Just look at him cum boys! Looks to me like what's happening to you here really gets your nut Detective."

My cargo of man juices landed all over my well-muscled chest, my nipples, my pecs, and dripped down to my stomach region.

"OHHHHHHHH," I groaned, looking up at the ceiling with my head tilted back, my goatee sopped in sweat. "I-I'm going to get you for this Wilkinson!!"

"Tell me Detective, how much is that wife of mine paying you to get the goods one me, as it would be said?" Wilkinson asked me snidely and let go of my cock as his two buddies lowered me to the floor but still held me tight by the upper arms.

My cock was tingling as it felt all spent at that moment...

"Th-that's confidential information between just her as my client and me," I ranted at him. "Mother fucker Wilkinson, *you just jacked me the fuck off like some cheap hustler on a Saturday night!!* And God almighty, even if you're planning to have your two goons here work me over I still won't tell you what your wife is paying me!!"

My cock tingled some more between my legs as it went semi soft and the last remnants of cum beaded at the tip of it. I had all to do to resist spitting in the guy's face as he stood there gloating, holding my underpants (of all things) in his hand... His two cronies leaned down at my fat fleshy nipples and slurped some of my cum off them.

"OHHHHHHH FUCK, I'm no goddamned faggot you bastards, get your mangy mouths off my man tits!!" I panted as they played chew and suck with my nipples.

My cock throbbed and I was sweaty in my sheers as I watched Wilkinson sniff my underpants again... My underpants...it was with them that all this had started...

When I had gotten back to my locker I stupidly failed to notice that my underpants were missing as I worked the combination lock on my locker. I always leave all my sweat soaked gear outside my locker on the floor while I go to shower after my workout, not wanting to stink up my suit and other clothes inside the locker. Of course I heard the stories of guys having their jockstraps and underpants snagged by other guys, but I never thought anyone would want mine. It's a sort of secret ritual among the sleazier sort of gay men I suppose, that by snagging their underpants or jockstrap you're showing them how much you like and appreciate their body. I had just put on my day old black ribbed calf length thick and thin sheer nylon socks and clipped my garters onto them when Wilkinson's two muscle buddies snuck up silently behind me. My sheers I always leave inside my locker crammed into my loafers. (My sheers are my personal favorites when it comes to my socks bud. My buddies at the police station tease me sometimes, calling me "the sheer socked detective." I suppose it sort of dates back to the detectives of the 1920's who always favored sheer socks and garters, perhaps I'm paying tribute to them in some way by wearing old fashioned sheers.) As I sat there on the bench in front of my locker looking around on the floor for my missing briefs the two big muscled goons grabbed my sore upper biceps and hauled me roughly to my feet.

"HHHHUUUUUUHHHHFFFFF!!!" I grunted in total surprise as my hairy tight butt left the bench, my semi hardness swinging back and forth in front of me, my hairy balls bobbing as I was hauled up just about to my socked tiptoes. "WH-what the fucking fuck???"

I involuntarily arched my hairy and muscled body forward as the two men hoisted me over the bench and put me down in the middle of the floor by my locker.

"Good evening Detective Neil," one of them said snidely.

As I got my bearings I looked longingly at my open locker and my suit jacket where I knew my gun was and then I saw Mr. Wilkinson appear from around the row of lockers. I didn't need three guesses to know what had happened. Fuck, somehow my cover had been blown and the guy had figured out that I was shadowing him, hired by his beautiful wife to prove he was cheating on her.

"Wilkinson!!!" I snarled through clenched teeth as his two muscle goons held me tight and fast up on my tiptoes.

"See you guys, I told you this detective dude knew who I was," the blond sleazy yet handsome man said as he sauntered over to us, my missing underpants in his hand.

I instantly regretted calling him by his name because *now* he knew for sure who *I was.* I suppose being caught by surprise I had let my guard down.

"Yeah, caught him off guard in just his sheer socks boss," the guy on my left said. "And just dig those garters he's got on, HA, just like a detective out of the roaring twenties."

"So glad you're a man after my own heart," I said to the guy with a sneer, quickly glancing at him and turning back to Wilkinson.

The two goons and Wilkinson laughed raucously, holding me tighter in their grasps.

"I'll bet this handsome detective has a sock fetish of some kind Mr. Wilkinson," the guy on my right said, and I then glanced at him angrily from the corner of my eye, again looking straight ahead at Mr. Wilkinson." Any guy who wears such sexy socks *with garters no less has to have a fetish I would think."*

"Takes one to know one," I mumbled under my breath, wiggling my toes in the solid black section of my sheers.

At the guy's mention of my sheer socks my cock bobbed to more than semi hard attention between my hairy and muscular legs and that was when Wilkinson brazenly took it in hand.

"OHHHHHHHH, G-GOD, call off your mugs, let go of my cock *and let me go man!!"* I ranted at him as he started stroking me.

"Let you go Detective Neil?" Wilkinson laughed, holding tight to my throbbing manhood. "But the fun is just getting started."

"Fun nothing you bastard!! There'll be other guys coming down to this stinking locker room to get changed man," I seethed at him through clenched teeth, chills speeding through me as he held my hardness tight, and my underpants in his other hand. "And when they do they'll see you perving all over me with my cock in your hand."

"Sorry to disappoint you Detective Neil," Wilkinson said and sniffed my underpants, stroking me at the same time. "But you were the last member here at the gym tonight. You were so into your workout that you failed to notice that. And you failed to notice my two buddies *shadowing you the way you've been shadowing me.* The gym is now officially closed for the night. My buddy there on your right is good friends with the gym instructor who was to lock the place up tonight."

"Yeah, I told him that I would lock the gym up for him tonight, once we saw you leave," the muscle guy on my right said with a sneer and gave my cheek a slurpy wet Bugs Bunny type of kiss. "Talk about a stroke of *sheer* luck huh Detective?"

"OHHHHHH FUCK, sleazy perv just kissed me, God almighty, and Wilkinson, let go of my damned cock man!!" I ranted.

"But obviously you won't be leaving all that soon Detective

Neil," Wilkinson said laughingly and stroked me some more.

"What the fuck Wilkinson???" I snarled at him as his two cronies hoisted me a few inches higher off the floor, my socked toes dangling just above the locker room carpet. "Fuckers, put me down!! And I have to get out of here man!! I got the wife waiting for me at home!!"

At that the three men laughed meanly, saying things like, "If your wife could see you now Detective!"

After I'd shot my load Wilkinson crammed my underpants in his pants pocket, (I supposed that he planned on keeping them as a souvenir of all this, God, how would I explain my missing underpants to the wife when I got home?? Fuck that, at the moment I had to concentrate first on getting the fuck home.) and then took a good long length of rope from a backpack he'd been carrying.

"Okay boys, lets get this sheer socked and gartered detective packaged," Wilkinson said and I cringed in fear as his buddies yanked my wrists in front of me and held them tightly together. "I plan to teach you to meddle in a man's private affairs Detective Sheers."

"Fucker, tying me up Wilkinson?" I panted as he bound my wrists tightly in front of me, the scent of my sweat mixed with cum emanating from my hairy muscular body.

"So am I right Detective Sheers?" the guy on my right asked me snidely as Wilkinson tied my wrists. "You got a sheer sock and garter fetish of some kind? 'Cause I got to tell you man, I'm straight as a fucking arrow but I sure do think that those big feet of yours look sexy as hell in your sheer socks, ha, ha, ha, ha, ha, ha, ha, ha!!!"

I clenched my teeth and watched miserably as Wilkinson wound and wound the rope around my wrists, knotting it as he went...

A few minutes later I was standing docilely still in just my sheers and garters as Wilkinson's muscled brutes wound a goodly length of rope over and over my upper torso, pulling the rope tight with each winding, pinning my arms to my body.

"Ah, bondage," Wilkinson said dreamily as his two cronies tied me and tied me, my lips pursed in out-right seething anger. "It can be so freeing wouldn't you say Detective Neil?"

"Freeing for you maybe bud," I bellowed at him. "But as the poor chump being roped up here I'm not feeling all that freed."

"Funny, my wife feels the same way, she just hates it when I want to play my kinky bondage games with her," Wilkinson sneered at me.

When the two muscle monsters were done tying my upper body I watched as Wilkinson took my attaché case from my locker.

"Don't touch that man!!" I ranted at him as his buddies squatted at my feet and tied them tightly together. "There's confidential information in there, *shit!!!*"

I looked down and saw Wilkinson's cronies playing "snap" with my sheer socks and garters as they squatted at my sides. I did my damnedest to stay balanced on my now tied feet... Wilkinson looked through the papers and folders of photographs in my attaché case, the photos of him with the mistress he had been fucking, the one I had been hired to prove he was having an affair with...GODS!!!

"Got it, got it," Wilkinson breathed, sounding relieved. "Now that wife of mine won't be able to prove a damned thing." With my lips pursed together in anger I watched, as the scumbag crammed my papers and the photographs into his backpack.

"You're good Detective, I'll give you that," Wilkinson laughed, stepping over to me and again grabbing my cock.

"OHHHHHHHH..." I gasped as he took me in hand and began stroking me a second time.

"Don't know how you were sly enough to get those pictures of me and the girlfriend, especially seeing as we were in a hotel room," Wilkinson said and stroked me faster, pulling me up to a new erection. "Now I wonder how you're going to explain your fuck-up and your capture to that wife of mine."

"BASTARD!!" I ranted at him and his buddies held me balanced by my upper arms as the guy stroked a second load of man juices from me. "OHHHHHHHH you fucker, got me spewing my damned load again, pervert!! Degenerate!!"

When I was done Wilkinson helped himself to my wallet that was in my suit jacket pocket, seeming not to care about my handgun that was also in there.

"Detective Neil Johnson," he said, holding up my ID card. "Well Detective Neil, you are officially off this case."

"That is not for you to decide Wilkinson," I spat at him as his two cronies grabbed my upper arms and hoisted me off the floor. "That's for your wife to decide bud…"

"What should we do with this guy boss?" one of Wilkinson's cronies asked as they held me aloft.

Wilkinson chuckled and I knew that his plans for me wouldn't be good…

"Lets tie him up to a post in the *ladies* locker room," Wilkinson laughed, taking some more rope out of his backpack. "No doubt when some fat biddy bitches get here in the morning for their workout and find him in there it'll be the best thing that's happened to them in a long time, and probably him as well, ha!!"

"Oh fuck, fuck," I prattled loudly as Wilkinson's two muscle cronies lugged me out of the men's locker room and to the ladies locker room, Wilkinson following with a goodly length of rope in hand…

The Next Morning…

"MMMFFFFFFF!!!" I grunted angrily behind the raunchy jockstrap gag that Wilkinson's muscle buddies had tied over my mouth as I stood there tied tightly to the post in the ladies locker room in just my sheer socks and garters.

Wilkinson had been right about the biddy bitches when they found me there the next morning… God almighty, but I was helpless as two of them alternately sucked my cock and played squeeze and tease with my nipples as well… Fuck, but I would have a lot of explaining to do to the wife… But inwardly, even as the horny housewives used me as a sex toy of sorts I knew that I had won. What Wilkinson didn't know was that I had copies of all the photographs and papers he stole from me in a safe deposit box… I tried to feel some semblance of triumph as the biddies feasted on me like a buffet…promising to untie me as soon as I shot one more load…just one more load…

The Wicked Story of Dr. Bottoms and Dan

Story inspired by: Franco's drawing, entitled "Doctor Bottomthrob's absolutely fiendish...Teasing and sucking and spanking machine.

"Well, it would certainly appear that everything in your medical facility and lab is in tiptop order Dr. Bottoms," the young handsome inspector said to me as we were just about to conclude his tour of the facility, the facility which I am in charge of.

"Yes, as you can see we do our best to keep everything in order and working and properly maintained," I said to the young man, holding his upper arm in a light grasp as we walked along.

He had his clipboard tucked under his other arm, finished with it at the moment and the taking of his notes.

"The students who come here to study and the patients that come here on their doctor's orders are all very much satisfied with our services Mr. Stevenson," I said to the inspector as we now made our way toward my private office. "My staff is very friendly and courteous to all who come here."

"Yes I saw that, your receptionist couldn't do enough for me when I got here," he said with a grin. "I got the feeling that she was a little nervous about my showing up unannounced and telling her that I was here for a surprise inspection."

"Not at all Mr. Stevenson," I said to him, gripping his arm tighter in a friendly manner, not wanting to tip the young man off to what I had in mind for him. "I think she became nervous because she found you to be so beguilingly handsome. I saw how the female staff members looked at you while we were touring and you were doing your inspection."

"Well now, that sure is flattering," the young man who looked a lot like Brad Pitt said and his face seemed to blush a light red. "Although I doubt that my fiancee' would want to hear that."

"Ah, you're getting married, lucky young man I'm sure," I said to him. "When is the big day?"

"A couple of months from now actually," he replied with a handsome and gracious smile, still blushing from the compliment I'd just paid him.

As we came to my office door I joined him in his nervous laughter and let go of his arm.

"Well, speaking for myself I must say that your fiancée is a lucky young lady," I said to the young man, opening my office door and ushering him inside. "You are not only handsome; you are intelligent and very committed to your job. I was able to tell that from the attention you paid to every thing I showed you during your inspection."

"Yeah, I guess I did at that," he said, looking down at his clipboard as we walked into my very spacious, very luxurious and very sound proofed office. "I worked hard to get this position so you know I'm going to do everything by the book."

"As you should, I said agreeably, stepping behind my desk as he stood by the chair that his suit jacket was hung neatly on the back of.

I had had him take off his suit jacket before the inspection, telling him to make himself as comfortable as possible. With a smile that could melt butter he agreed.

"So I think we covered just about everything," he said, looking up at me from his clipboard as I sat down behind my desk. "Except for whatever is in that room."

He pointed to the door behind my desk, the door to the only room I hadn't brought him in during his surprise inspection. It was at that very moment that I was overjoyed that Mr. Dan Stevenson was nosy, too nosy for his own good, for it was in that room that I planned to punish the young man for springing this inspection on me and my unsuspecting staff. Even though I was sure that it was his superiors that wanted my facility inspected, it was to be handsome Dan Stevenson who would pay dearly for the surprise brought upon my staff and I.

"Oh, that room?" I replied, trying to sound as dumb as possible. "That's nothing you need to see for your inspection."

"Ah, ah, ah, Dr. Bottoms," the young man said, wagging a finger at me. "You said that I do everything by the book and that is what I intend to do."

I smiled at him and shrugged.

"Now, let me see what you have tucked away in there and then I'll be on my way, with a glowing report about your facility I might add," he said, looking intently at me with those crystal blue killer eyes of his.

Still smiling I rose to my feet and took a set of keys out of my top desk drawer. The young man stepped behind me as I opened the door. He followed me inside like a puppy following his master. As I locked the door behind us the young inspector was automatically, practically instantly transfixed by what he saw in the epicenter of the room. Slowly, he made his way over to the machine, my own creation; my device if you would…

"What is this thing?" Dan Stevenson asked me, tucking his clipboard again under his arm as he looked the machine over, circling it, a look of more than curiosity etched on his handsome face.

"It's a creation of mine Mr. Stevenson," I replied, sounding bored. "It's used for a variety of reasons."

What Mr. Stevenson was taking in the sight of was my spanking machine. Actually, what were visible to him were only the spanking devices. The rest of the machinery was safely out of sight, until it was turned on that is. The machine was really an old workout horse that I had taken from the gym. Attached to the sides of the horse were two heavy-duty plastic rounded attachments, for the recipient's legs to be encased in. On the sides of those were two long wooden strips of wood with wrist bonds at the end of them. In the center of the long pieces of wood was two leather spanking paddles attached to spindles, aimed directly over where the recipient's bottom would be. In the center of the workout horse, hidden underneath the thing was a long leather strap, used to fasten the recipient's upper torso to the horse. Dead center of the horse was a hole, cheerfully called a glory hole by myself. The hole was used to wedge the male member through, although the handsome male inspecting my machine at the moment had no idea just what the hole was for. He would soon though, if everything went the way I hoped it would, *he soon would know*. Under the workout horse was my milking attachment, complete in the dead center with a latex tube shaped lubricated suction device. At the moment the suction device was hidden from view, down in the bowels of the suction machine. On the sides of the suction machine were two metal ankle restraints for keeping the recipients feet spread wide.

"Used for a variety of reasons?" the young inspector, asked me, squatting down at the side of the thing, running his fingers over one of the ankle restraints.

"Well yes, I use it on patients to test their nerve endings," I explained.

"Huh?" the young man replied, looking up at me with bewilderment showing in his eyes.

"Well, after a certain age the nerve endings cease to function correctly," I explained. "The devices on this machine stimulate those nerve endings, hopefully getting a reaction. Do you understand?"

"I'm not sure," the inspector said, putting his clipboard down on the floor and squatting still closer to the device. "What else is it used for?"

"Well, in certain recipients it's used to test endurance levels," I explained. "That's for the younger recipients, not the older ones that I just mentioned."

"What kind of endurance testing Dr. Bottoms?" the young man asked me, getting to his feet. "And please be specific."

"Well, it would be easier to explain if I had a recipient in the device," I said, looking toward the door. "Perhaps I could ask one of my staff members to give you a demonstration. The control panel for the device is in that booth behind that glass partition."

He looked at where I was pointing and looked back at me.

"There's no need to get a staff member Dr. Bottoms," he said to me sounding cross all of a sudden. "I'm here after all. If I had to I wouldn't mind being in the machine while you demonstrate it for me."

"Oh, so then you won't want a demonstration after all," I said, trying to make it sound like this was the end of the discussion concerning my machine.

"Oh I want the demonstration Dr. Bottoms," Mr. Stevenson said sternly. "My curiosity about this thing is genuinely piqued."

"Well then, you'll have to follow my instructions," I said, sounding concerned.

"I'm prepared," he said. "My managers wanted this place inspected from top to bottom Doctor. I don't intend to leave one stone unturned."

He placed his hands on his hips, took a deep breath and looked at me sternly.

"What do I have to do?" he asked me.

I think that the fact that he thought he was giving orders to a man older than he was, was very ego boosting for him. Given the chance and if this went the way I was praying it would I would soon teach him a lesson where his overly inflated ego was concerned.

"Well, for starters you need to undress down to your underwear," I said, sounding as sheepish as possible.

The inspector gulped but still began undoing his necktie.

"Down to my underwear eh?" he asked me, sliding his tie off his crisp white shirt and holding it in hand as it dangled.

"Yes, its best that way when the recipient is in the machine, it's exactly like a medical exam where you have to disrobe for your doctor," I said, stammering purposely and trying to sound as foolish as possible. "But Mr. Stevenson, this is not necessary..."

"Well, I told my manager that I would do whatever was necessary for the job when he dangled it in front of my face," the young man said with a grin. But stripping didn't enter my mind at that time. But what the hey right? We're both guys here after. I'll just be another pretty face for you right Doc? I'm sure throughout your long career you've seen lots of guys stripped to their underwear. And just for the record Doctor Bottoms, it's completely necessary."

My long career, I did not like his reference to my age, not one bit. As he undressed I brought a chair out for him from the control booth. He neatly stacked his clothes on the chair.

"Mr. Stevenson, if you're uncomfortable about this I will gladly bring in a student recipient to demonstrate the machine for you," I insisted. "There really is no need for all this, I assure you."

"No, no, it's part of my job as an inspector to inspect," he said, unbuttoning his suit pants. "And you are a doctor after all so this really is no big deal, right? I've been to the doctor countless times. Not to mention that I've changed my clothes in front of total strangers countless times in a locker room as well. No, it isn't a problem at all. Besides, I get paid very well for the job I do."

He sounded more like he was trying to convince himself of all he was saying. I doubted very much that he ever thought that this would be part of his job as a facility inspector.

"The things a guy has to do for his job," the young man said, stepping out of his navy blue suit pants after having taken off his black shiny lace-up wing tips.

A few moments later he was standing beside the device clad in just his white BVD briefs and calf length navy blue nylon dress socks, Gold Toe brand, a real favorite with these young executives. My heart was racing. I could not believe my luck, nor could I believe the young man's gullibility.

"Okay, what now?" he asked, obviously feeling very embarrassed even though he was in the presence of a doctor.

The young man not only looked like Brad Pitt, but his body

was as exquisite as Brad Pitt's was as well. He had a muscular and exquisitely defined upper torso, chiseled and solidly toned. His shoulders were muscular and broad, his biceps and triceps bulging. His chest was muscular, smooth and adorned with two very pointy very brown fleshy nipples. I imagined his fiancée having the time of her life with those nipples of his. His legs were long and muscular, what would be called tree trunks-like legs. From the slight bulge I saw in his white briefs I gathered that he was greatly gifted in that area. We would soon find out I thought happily, if I were able to keep this charade going that is.

"Well now, I have to get you hooked up to the machine and then I'll be able to give you a demonstration," I said to the young man as he nervously curled his toes back under his socks.

"So you mean that I have to lie down in this thing, put my legs in those rounded plastic holders huh?" he asked me, stepping with me closer to the machine.

"I'll help you to get positioned properly Mr. Stevenson," I said. "One good boost should have you in there just right."

That said I quickly and without permission took the young man by his mid section, wrapping my strong arms around him. I hoisted him up off the floor and held him prone over the machine.

"*Wh-whoa,* y-you're sure a lot stronger than you look Dr. Bottoms," the young man said as I hoisted him into position over the machine. "I'm nearly two hundred pounds of sheer muscle and you just lifted me like I weighed nothing."

"All part of staying is shape Mr. Stevenson," I huffed, lowering my victim into the device.

"Yeah, got me all stretched out in a Superman flying position here huh?" the young man said with a sexy grin on his face. "Even my trainer at the gym wouldn't be able to lift me like this Doc. All those years of keeping in shape huh? Good for you Dr. Bottoms."

Again that reference to my age that I truly resented. I took solace in the fact that very soon the young man would be suffering his punishment for his arrogance.

"Oh yes Mr. Stevenson, nothing like a lifelong and routine exercise regiment to keep one fit and strong," I said as I positioned him over the machine.

"Huh, I got to say Doctor that this is has turned out to be the craziest inspection I've ever conducted," Dan Stevenson said as I lowered him onto the device.

As soon as he was in the device and splayed I instantly got to work fastening his wrists to the wooden strips of wood at the sides of the device.

"Hey, don't secure me in here too tight," he said, sounding very nervous at that point. "I'm going to need my hands free to take notes after all."

But it was too late. His hands were now tightly fastened to the machine and spread wide. Without a word I brought out the unseen straps and secured his legs at the thighs and knees. His skin felt like silk to put it plainly.

"Hey Doc, what's up with those straps on my legs?" he asked, sounding extremely nervous now. "Y-you didn't mention them before."

"All for the purposes of the demonstration Mr. Stevenson," I explained, squatting down at one of his dangling socked feet.

He turned and watched as I took his right-sided foot by his socked ankle and guided it perilously into the restraint. A look of bewilderment crossed his handsome face as I took a hearty sniff of his socked foot. It smelled musty and raw to put it plainly. The young man smiled a bit embarrassingly.

"I know about that thing where my smelly socks are concerned Doctor," he said, trying to make idle conversation, despite the position he was now in. "My fiancée refuses to handle my socks. She makes me put them right into the washing machine when I take them off at the end of the day."

"You don't say," I replied, giving his foot a squeeze after securing it into the restraint.

I quickly dashed over to his other foot…

"Yeah, she says that I must have the worst smelling feet in the world," he went on as I took his left-sided foot in hand as I had done with his other one, sniffing it before securing it into the ankle restraint.

"Well, perhaps I'll refer you to a good foot doctor after we're done here," I suggested. "I know someone who specializes in the problem of smelly feet."

He was obviously telling me about his fiancée and his smelly feet to avoid mentioning the fact that I had sniffed his socked feet, bad as they smelled. After I was done securing his feet in the restraints I stood up straight and stepped to his right side.

"Okay, that looks just about right I would say," rubbing my chin as if I was in deep thought. "But still, one thing needs to be adjusted."

"Wh-what's that Doc?" the young man asked me, looking up at me apprehensively.

"Well, your penis should be pulled behind your buttocks and between your thighs and brought through the hole cut into the workout horse that you're straddling," I replied.

"Huh?" he asked, nearly gasping. "*N-now wait a minute here Doc…*"

"I'll have to snip those under shorts of yours off you Mr. Stevenson," I said, taking a pair of sharp-edged surgical scissors from my lab coat pocket. "You do want to experience my device correctly after all."

"H-hey now, wait just a goddamned second here man," he garbled angrily as I carefully began snipping his underpants off him. "D-don't be taking my underpants off me you crazy doctor! And fuck man, just what the hell are you planning on doing with my goddamned joystick?"

I had to chuckle softly at the way he referred to his penis as his joystick. When his underpants were snipped down the middle I managed to slide them off him. He squirmed miserably as they came off him and he looked even angrier as I deposited them into the pocket of my lab coat.

"Stealing my damned stinking underpants man?" he asked me. "Fuck man but that's a shitty and perverted thing to do to a guy!"

Smiling, I stepped between his splayed legs, reached between them and not all that gently brought out his oversized "joystick" along with two of the biggest and juiciest balls I had ever handled.

"Ohhhhhhrrrr, uhhhhhhnnnn, ea-easy with my joystick you bastard," he snarled as I guided his semi hardness through the glory hole, resting his kiwi sized balls atop the back of the work-out horse.

His penis was long enough to have his balls rest comfortably or perhaps not so comfortably atop the horse. I rubbed a finger against his balls, loving the velvety feel of the peach fuzz covering them.

"Hmmmm, are you sure you're more than twenty years old or so Mr. Stevenson?" I asked him, gliding my finger over his balls. "This peach fuzz says eighteen or nineteen to me."

"Fucker!!" he garbled at me, looking back at me. "L-let me off this monstrosity! I've changed my mind!"

He went to try to lift his buttocks up to get his penis out of the glory hole but I quickly pushed him back down and then tightened the restraints around his torso and his thighs, now totally immobilizing him. No way could he get his manhood out of the hole now.

"*You bastard*," he whispered as I lovingly caressed his smooth as silk bubble shaped butt, giving it a handful of a squeeze as well.

I took note of the fact that his manhood swelled in the glory hole, causing it to bob and twitch back and forth. I picked up his clipboard and stood next to his handsome face as he looked up at me.

"I suppose I'll have to take notes for you now Mr. Stevenson," I said with a wicked looking grin on my face. "Seeing as you're all tied up at the moment, and will be for quite some time."

"Qu-quite some time?" he grumbled through trembling lips. "Just how long do you plan on keeping me like this?"

As he complained bitterly I cupped his chin in my hand, caressing it, stroking it.

"Well, most recipients of your age usually endure any-where from two to four hours of my machine," I said to him.

"*Two to four hours?*" he squeaked.

"But in your case seeing as we have the entire afternoon ahead of us I would think that five or six hours is acceptable," I said, took my hand off his chin and walked toward the control booth.

"F-five or six hours?" he barked at me. "You plan to keep me here like this for that long? You can't!"

"And why not?" I asked him, turning around and looking at him.

"I-I have other appointments, other inspections to be at," he explained in fear.

"It is much more important that you inspect my machine Mr. Stevenson," I said, pointing at him, a stern look now etched on my face. "I want a glowing report from you when we're done here."

"You bastard! Let me off this thing!" he roared at me as I stepped into the control booth and looked at him through the window.

"This booth is equipped with a two way speaker system Mr. Stevenson," I said to him, speaking into the small microphone in front of me. "Anything you say can be heard by me and obvi-ously what I'm saying can be heard out there by you."

He looked up at me miserably and I swear he looked as if he was about to cry.

"Let me go Dr. Bottoms!" he snarled through clenched teeth. "I'm going to tell my superiors about this!"

"I should hope so Mr. Stevenson," I replied. "But do you think you really would want to tell them how you voluntarily had me install you into my machine?"

"I-I'll tell them you tricked me!" he replied loudly.

"An intelligent young man like yourself?" I asked him and placed my hand on the knob that controlled the spindles that supported the spanking paddles. "Your curiosity has gotten you in deeper than you thought you could ever have imagined. Now Mr. Stevenson enough of this prattle. It's time to begin the demonstration."

That said I turned the knob and the spindles came to life, slowly at first rotating the paddles. The paddles connected with each spin against Dan Stevenson's sexy buttock cheeks, spanking them stingingly.

"H-hey, now wait, just hold on here," the young man blurted, craning his head and looking back as the machine did its dirty work. "Th-those fucking things are spanking my ass!" "Precisely Mr. Stevenson," I said and turned the knob some more, increasing the speed on the spindles.

"Owwwwwwwww!!! Oh geez, you crazy doctor!" the inspector snarled, turning his head and looking up at me in the booth.

"The way I usually do this with other recipients is that I spank them for a good twenty minutes to a half hour or so before milking them," I said to him as the spindles spun and spun and spanked and spanked the Brad Pitt look-a-like.

"M-milk them? Owwwwwrrrr!!! Just what the fuck is that supposed to mean?" he asked me miserably as his sweet butt cheeks were already turning red.

Obviously he had very sensitive skin.

I turned the knob some more and the spindles spun even faster, whacking his butt cheeks harder and harder.

"Owwwww!!!" he snarled.

Then, to answer his question I pushed a button on the control panel. From the depths of the attached device under the workout horse the latex tube shaped device slid upwards and into view, not into my victim's view however. The much lubricated tube encased itself around Mr. Stevenson's erect penis and when I pushed another button it closed tight around it.

"Ohhhhhrrrr f-fuck, wh-what is that?" he grumbled. "OWWWWWWW!!! Fucking things man, spanking the very tar out of me!"

"That Mr. Stevenson is the milking device," I explained to

him as the tube hugged his penis. "After you've been spanked for a good amount of time I will turn on the suction on that thing. By the time the afternoon is over I'll have you shooting dry loads, mark my words."

"F-fuck man, that could drive a guy crazy," he whimpered as I released the tube and made it slide off his erection. "uhhhhhh, b-but that did feel great for a second you bastard! OWWWWWWWWW!!!!"

I turned the knob one last time, bringing the spindles up to full spinning capacity. They were spinning now at high speed and the sounds of Mr. Stevenson's buttocks being spanked repeatedly filled the room. He gasped, yelped and thrashed on my device.

"F-fucker!!" he snarled meanly as I stepped out of the control booth and over to him, his clipboard and pen in hand.

"The spindles rotate at better than eighty to ninety revolutions per minute Mr. Stevenson, I said to the young man, writing the information on his yellow pad on the clipboard. "That means that each of your cheeks is being paddled at least that many times each minute."

"Owwwwwwrrrr!!!" the young victim howled and the sounds of the spindles spanking his butt cheeks seemed to intensify some more. "An-and this is for endurance testing? Shit, *shit!! Oww!!!*"

"Well, besides testing nerve endings and endurance levels I also use the machine as a device for punishment purposes," I explained, writing and writing on his clipboard.

"Punishment purposes?" he asked me angrily. "What the fuck does that mean? Owwwwwwwwww!!! Please man, turn it off already!!"

"Well, I want all the students who come here to do well Mr. Stevenson, my reputation depends on that," I said, ruffling his wavy light brown hair as he hung there on the device. "And I've noticed through the years that the male students give me the most problems when it comes to their studies."

"So, so, arrrrghhhh shit, so you use this thing to keep them in line?" my victim asked in disbelief.

"Precisely," I replied, sounding like a proud father. "When they sign on to study under me they sign an agreement to punishment should they shirk their academic duties."

"Owwwww fuccckkk man, th-this is awful," the inspector grumbled. "Owwwwwww!!!! Shiiitttt!!! Ev-even my dad never spanked me this badly."

"H-how many students have you punished in this fashion Dr. Bottoms?" Dan Stevenson asked me through clenched teeth.

"As luck would have it for the students not that many," I replied, again cupping his chin in my hand and caressing it lovingly. "You see, the first time I punished a young man for failing an exam I had his buddies in here to watch his humiliation. After that most of the students stayed in line. But of course there are always the ones who downfall."

"Pl-please, let me off this thing man," he sniveled as I stroked his chin, tears forming in his eyes. "I've had enough for the demonstration."

"Had enough?" I asked him, sounding astonished and let go of his chin. "Why Mr. Stevenson, we've hardly begun."

Standing there I watched as the young man writhed miserably, hung perilously and helplessly in my device. His muscles in his back, his arms and his legs rippled and squirmed exquisitely. He opened and closed his hands into and out of fists. His toes curled back under his socks and his penis was as hard as steel in the glory hole. Already his butt cheeks were a nice shade of red. They twitched after each spank they endured and his balls suffered beautifully atop the horse and under his splayed thighs.

"I-I'll have your medical license revoked for this," he seethed at me. "Fucking pervert! You can't do this to your students and you can't do this to me!"

"Ah, but with all due respect Mr. Stevenson," I chuckled meanly. "I am doing it to you."

He looked at me and grimaced, screeched in pain and the sounds of the spinning paddles connecting over and over and over with his rump filled the room. He watched helplessly as I wrote notes on his clipboard.

"OWWWWWWW!!!!" he roared madly. "G-God almighty, th-the way I'm screaming like a banshee why doesn't someone come?"

"This whole room including my outer office is totally soundproof Mr. Stevenson," I explained. "I had it built that way when the lab was first brought into existence."

Again he looked at me miserably.

"Next time you'll think twice about springing a surprise inspection on a doctor of my stature," I said to him, showing my anger now.

"It, it wasn't my decision man!" he yelped at me desperately as I walked slowly back to the control room. "*I was sent here on assignment.*"

"And you are on assignment Mr. Stevenson," I said to him, turning and pointing a finger at my machine as it spanked and spanked and spanked him. "Consider that machine part of your assignment."

With that I stepped back into the control room…

I watched through the glass for a good fifteen more minutes while the young handsome man suffered madly through the spanking he was getting… Needless to say that like him I was hard as steel…

At the end of the first half-hour I slowly turned the knob backward, slowly, so slowly making the spindles stop.

"Owwwwwwww!!!" the young inspector continued to whimper however.

As I slowed the spindles down I pressed the button that controlled the tube shaped latex lubricated milking device. The thing slid up from the bowels of the machine, alive and sucking, alive and hungry for some young inspector's cock. It engulfed the young man's penis and when I pressed another button it hugged the member tight.

"Ayyyyrrrr, wh-what are you doin' to me here man?" the young man blurted, his head snapping up and he looking at me in wonderment.

I stopped the spindles completely, ending his first round of spanking. His butt cheeks were a nice shade of red already. Smiling at him I pressed another button on the control panel and the suction device around his big erect penis began slowly sliding up and down his shaft.

"Ohhhhhhhh, oh Doc, ohhhhrrr f-fuck," he stammered in the forced ecstasy. "Ohhhhrrr yeah, fucking thing is sucking my joystick man!"

The combination of the latex material and the lubricant that was soaked into it was enough to send the young candidate into a deep and heated sexual frenzy. He bucked like crazy on the machine, clenching and unclenching his fists, curling his toes back under his blue socks and sweating like crazy.

"Ohhhhhrrr fuuucckkk, y-you're going to make me cream my load like crazy Doc," the young man gasped, looking at me through the glass.

I simply nodded, a look of glee etched on my face.

"So tell me Mr. Stevenson, what do you think of the demonstration so far?" I asked him.

"I-I have to say that I'm overwhelmed Doc," he responded and I quickly jotted some notes on his clipboard. "Hoo whee, I wonder if having your machine sucking my joystick would be considered cheating on my fiancée."

I nearly broke out in peals of laughter as he said that.

"After you've shot your first load I'll have the paddles revved up again for another half hour or so of spanking fun," I said to him and he just looked at me blankly. "Now, are you still thinking about your other appointments Mr. Stevenson?"

"I-I really should be on my way at this poi---ohhhhrrr fuccckkkkk," the young man began to say, but it was at that very moment that the suction device began sucking his first load from him. "Ohhhhrrr, I-I'm creaming Doc, I'm fucking shooting my wad!"

I increased the suction pressure on the tube shaped cylinder, forcing the young man further into blinding ecstasy. His load of sperm was sucked from him and deposited in the clear tube on the bottom and outside of the machine. Glee filled me as I watched his soup end up in the tube.

"Ohhhhhhrrrr f-fuck, got to admit man, it feels awesome," he panted. "F-fucking thing is driving me crazy!"

He seemed to cum and cum, shooting glob after glob of his potent mess. I hastily jotted notes on his clipboard and fleetingly wondered if this was how potent he was with his fiancée. Nah, it had to be my machine that was causing it. When he was done I pressed the reverse button and the suction device released his penis and slowly slid off it. He was still breathless as the thing slid off him. His penis remained trapped in the glory hole all slimy looking now and his balls seemed to be heaving atop the horse, obviously still chock filled with more of his precious juices. I quickly turned the knob that controlled the spindles. Slowly, the sounds of spanking and the young man's yelps of pain and humiliation again filled the room.

"Owwwwwwww!!! *Shit, shit,* don't be spanking me again man!" he pleaded helplessly. "Goddamn it, what's the point of all this anyhow?"

"The point Mr. Stevenson is to prove that a thorough spanking can make a man more than hard and beyond potent," I replied from inside the booth. "Those paddles spanking your sweet butt cheeks are made of leather, stinging leather I might add."

"Yeah, owwwwww!!! S-so I've noticed," the young man quipped miserably. "Never really thought of my goddamned butt cheeks as sweet though Doc."

"Ten to fifteen minutes of being continuously spanked with leather paddles can more than drive a man crazy," I said. "I'm going to give you another half hour and then some."

"N-no!!" he blurted, looking up at me helplessly through the glass.

Smiling meanly at him I opened a drawer on the control panel and took out the device that I planned to drive him mad with next. The device was a stainless steel golf ball-sized vibrator with a thin wire attached to it. On the side of the vibrator/ball was a switch. With the device in hand I stepped out of the booth and walked over to my latest recipient.

"So, how are you enjoying the demonstration so far Mr. Stevenson?" I asked him as the poor young man was spanked and spanked and spanked.

"Uhhhhhrrrrrr, j-just fucking grand you crazy doctor," he replied sarcastically. "J-just what I've always wanted, to be spanked while wearing just my damned stinking socks!"

"Glad to hear it, because now I'm going to take you to the next level," I said, holding up the vibrator/ball for him to see.

"Wh-what's that thing?" he asked me, sounding fearful.

Smiling, I put the device temporarily into my lab coat pocket along with his underpants. From the other side pocket I took out a small tube of KY lubricant. I stepped behind the young man, took the cap off the tube and placed the tip of it against his ass-crack.

"H-hey, wh-what the hell are you doing back there?" he grumbled, trying to crane his head around to see what I was doing.

I squeezed the tube and a good dollop of KY lubricant slathered the walls and deep crevices of his hole.

"OOOOOOO, WH-what are you doin' to me here Doc?" he asked breathlessly as I screwed the cap back onto the tube, putting the tube back in my pocket. "OWWWWWWW!!!! Fucking things spanking me are driving me crazy man!! F-fuck, how am I going to explain red butt cheeks to my fiancée?"

"Heh, does she check your butt cheeks every night Mr. Stevenson?" I asked him and took the vibrator/ball out of my pocket.

He grimaced in misery and then I slowly inserted the ball/vibrator into his hole, leaving the switch part of it visible.

"WH-what are you doing?" he asked in a high pitched tone of voice as the walls of his hole hugged the thing. *"Oh God, wh-what are you doing?"*

I carefully tied the thin wire around his bulging balls, making them look real swollen.

"The device that I just inserted in your anus is a battery operated vibrator ball Mr. Stevenson," I explained. "The current is light but in a moment when I switch it on you're going to feel a definite tingling in your hole, and in your big juicy balls back here."

"N-no, no, don't turn that thing on man, I swear to God you'll pay for this," he garbled crazily. "OWWWW!!! Turn off the spankers man, please! *You will pay for all of this!*"

"Send the bill to my secretary," I laughed and flicked the small switch on the device on.

"Ohhhhhrrrrrrr, ohhhhrrr fuck, it-it feels like you're cooking my hole and my balls!" he gasped.

"The combination of being spanked and having your hole and balls electrically stimulated will no doubt have you hard as steel very soon Mr. Stevenson," I said, stepping to his head and ruffling his beautiful wavy hair. "I'm sure you'll be pleading with me to let you shoot another load before I stop the spindles the second time."

I smiled wickedly down at him and made my way back to the control booth...

"Fucker, pervert," he ranted angrily at my back. "God almighty, now you've really got me going crazy Doc!"

"If your fiancée could see you now Mr. Stevenson," I laughed and stepped back into the control booth.

"Yeah right, she wouldn't believe it," he grumbled. "Fuck it all, *I don't believe it!*"

It was fifteen minutes later and Mr. Stevenson's cock was again rock hard in the glory hole of the horse he was splayed and secured on. The constant sounds of the leather paddles, thwacking against his now very crimson butt cheeks continued to fill the air. His cries of anger, rage and out-right humiliation also went on and on.

"B-bastard, I swear I'll get you for this!" the young inspector croaked, looking up at me and then lowering his head. "OWWWWWWW, of all the blasted things!!"

At this point he was having a difficult time of it keeping his head held straight out. Because of the position I had him in there really was no support for his head. He was matted from head to toe in sweat at that point. With his clipboard in hand I again stepped out of the control booth and walked over the sweating, swearing and whimpering Dan Stevenson.

"L-let me off this wretched thing already," he snuffled as I walked past him.

Ignoring his request I stepped behind him to observe his big juicy cock and his bulging balls. The sound of the ball/vibrator humming in his hole was music to my ears. His crimson butt cheeks were awash with goose bumps from the constant hum in his anus and around his balls. As I expected I found his penis to be harder than it was the first time I'd milked him. He was in a definite state of ecstasy and pain all at the same time.

"Very nice Mr. Stevenson," I said gleefully, trailing a fingertip across his peach-fuzzed balls.

They felt alive to the touch, twitching and pulsing in his sexy sac. The current from the wire tied around them made them a little warm. I couldn't help thinking of hot roasted nuts. Droplets of pre cum oozed from his slit and landed on the machine under him.

"Hmmm, looks like I'll have to be milking you again pretty soon Mr. Stevenson," I said to him, applying slight pressure to his heated balls with my fingertip.

"Ohhhhhh, fuccccckkk, lea-leave my damned balls alone you crazy doctor!" he sputtered.

"Tell me Mr. Stevenson, and answer truthfully or risk me not turning off the spindles in another ten minutes or so," I said to him. "Are you feeling just a tad horny at the moment?"

He gulped hard, whimpered at the pain being inflicted on his buttocks and craned his head as far as possible to try to look at me.

"I-I'm so fucking worked up that I can't believe it man," he grunted. "OWWWWWWW, fucking paddles! I-I'm no faggot Doctor Bottoms, but that thing you got stuck in my ass in driving me batty!"

I smiled, made a few notes on his clipboard and slowly walked along side him, making my way back to the control room.

"I-I answered truthfully Doc," he stammered as I walked by him.

"Oh I know, I know," I said, turning to look at him. "I know..."

I walked back into the control booth and opened the drawer under the control panel. This time I took out a pair of sharp-teethed tit clamps.

"Another ten minutes Mr. Stevenson and then I'll stop the spindles again and commence milking you," I said.

"G-gee thanks Doc," he replied sarcastically.

Ten minutes later I slowly turned the knob that controlled the spanking spindles to the off position. As the spindles slowed down the young man breathed easier and sighed with relief. Smiling, I pressed the button that controlled the tube shaped suction device. The slimy and lubricated thing slid up from the bowels of the machine and enveloped young Mr. Stevenson's pulsing hard penis.

"Ohhhh fuck, goddamned thing loves my joystick Doc," he grumbled as I pressed the button that got the thing moving up and down his shaft, slowly sucking him. "Oh fuck, it-it's tighter than my fiancée's damned pussy!"

"Tell me about your fiancé, Mr. Stevenson," I said sternly, my finger poised over the button that would slide the suction device off the young man's penis.

"Oh man Doc, she-she's awesome, beautiful girl," he began as the thing sucked him and sucked him. "God, just think-ing about her while that thing eats my joystick is enough to make me cream my load...ohhhh yeah, I-I'm goin' to cum now man!!"

But just as his orgasm began I quickly pressed the button that made the suction device slide off his penis.

"I-I-ohhhhhrrrr f-fuck, wh-what'd you do that for man?" he grumbled at me, his head raised. "Geez, I-I can't cum now!!!"

He writhed and bucked madly in the restraints, his penis twitching and his big balls bulging with his juices.

"Just as I thought," I said. "Depriving you of the orgasm is worse torture than being spanked."

"Fuck man, but that's a shitty thing to do to a guy," he yelled angrily. "G-get that damned thing back on my joystick and make it suck me off Doc!"

"What was that you just asked Mr. Stevenson?" I asked my recipient, a twinkle in my eyes as he looked up at me help-lessly.

"I-I can't believe I just asked you for that man, but shit, this thing cooking my hole and my balls is too much now!!" he garbled, tears in his eyes.

"Perhaps after another good half-hour or so of being spanked Mr. Stevenson I'll let you cum," I said and slowly turned the knob that controlled the spanking spindles. "Or perhaps I won't!"

"Oh no, no, don't be spanking me again, please man," the young inspector pleaded. "Oh God, just how long do you plan on keeping me here like this???"

"Now Mr. Stevenson, you already know the answer to that question," I replied sadistically.

I revved up the spindles to full power... In seconds the handsome young man was crying and crying...

"F-fucker..." he sputtered angrily, spittle flying from his trembling lips.

He writhed, bucked and was a sweaty mess on my machine. I leaned back in my chair in the control booth and jotted notes on his clipboard...

It was forty-five minutes later when I slowly shut the spindles off again... For the last twenty minutes or so the young man hadn't lifted his head. He had simply hung there on the machine whimpering gasping and swearing like a marine as the paddles spun and spanked his glorious ass cheeks.

"Forty five minutes you endured that time Mr. Stevenson," I said as I stepped out of the control room. "So far all totaled you've seen my machine work for an hour and forty five minutes. That's a hell of a lot of time for a man to be spanked I would say."

"Yeah, I would say that too," the young man said wearily, lifting his head and looking at me beseechingly. "Pl-please Doc, the demonstration was awesome. But please, let me off this thing now."

"Not just yet Mr. Stevenson," I said, holding up a jar of aloe skin cream. "I still want to see what the effects of my milking machine have on you...after I've allowed you to cum again that is."

Stepping behind him and between his splayed thighs I took the lid off the jar of the skin cream. His butt cheeks were beyond fire engine red at that point. They were crimson and I swear they were twitching with a life all their own. What a lovely sight that was I must say. The ball/vibrator buzzed and buzzed in his hole, cooking his anus and making his balls swell more and more. The young man seemed to have more than a few potent loads in him, judging from the size of his throbbing balls. Even after I'd had my machine suck that first load out of him he was ready for more.

"Now, I don't want these exquisite butt cheeks of yours to start bleeding at all while you're enduring the next spanking sessions so I'll just moisten them up a bit for you," I said.

With that said I spread a few good globs of the cream over his silky and hot to the touch crimson cheeks.

"Oooooooo, got to admit, that feels real soothing Doc," he exclaimed as I kneaded the cream over and over his sweet cheeks.

"Really?" I asked him, pressing a finger against the ball/vibrator in his hole. "And how is this baby making you feel at this point?"

"It, it's making me crazy Doc," he replied breathlessly. "I'm sweating like a real football jock here."

I took a deep breath and agreed with him. The air in the room smelled of sweat, hot musty young male sweat. Even the scent from his sweat soaked socks filled the air. No doubt the young man would need to shower before he left the facility. I smeared more of the cream over his reddened butt cheeks and even smeared some over his throbbing shaft as it hung there long and hard in the glory hole.

"Ohhhhrrrr yeah, yeah, fucking get me off you pervert," he seethed as I teasingly stroked his manhood.

I stroked him slowly a few times and even poked the tip of a finger into his pre cum slopped slit. He moaned and groaned about how good it felt and begged and pleaded for me to get him off. He exclaimed how he was getting close and was about to shoot his load. But then agony when I took my hand off it.

"Ohhhhhh no, no, fucker, let me cum," he pleaded miserably.

I screwed the top back onto the jar of aloe cream, placed the jar on top of the machine under him and stepped in front of the handsome and delectable young inspector.

"Y-you fucking bastard, milking me that first time got me all worked up, now look at me!" he grunted miserably.

"Now, before I start the spindles again I have one more adjustment to make," I said and took the tit clamps out of my pocket.

"Wh-what are those for?" he asked through trembling lips as I squeezed them open.

"Why Mr. Stevenson, you've obviously led a very sheltered life," I said with that twinkle in my eye. "Haven't you ever heard of tit clamps?"

"N-no," he stammered as I reached under him and clipped the tit clamps onto his big fleshy nipples.

"Ayyyyrrrrrrr!!!" he seethed. "Oh, but those things smart you bastard!"

He lifted his torso as high as possible and I can't tell you how pretty a picture he made with those clamps dangling off his nipples. In seconds his nips were being squeezed up to twice their normal size.

"Okay Mr. Stevenson, that's enough break time for now," I

said, ruffling his hair. "It's time to start the demonstration again."

"N-no, d-don't spank me again man, please!!" he begged. "God almighty, these things on my nipples and that fucking thing you got wedged in my stinking hole are making me crazy Doc!!"

Smiling, I stepped into the control booth.

"I'm glad to hear that Mr. Stevenson," I said merrily. "It means that what I want to demonstrate for you is working."

He looked at me in misery through the glass and I placed my hand on the knob that controlled the spindles. I gave it a slow turn to the on position and watched as again the spindles started rotating, spanking the inspector's butt cheeks. Smiling meanly, I turned the knob some more and the speed of the spindles increased.

"Ayyyyrrrrrrrr!!!" Dan Stevenson whimpered loudly.

I watched as the aloe cream that I had rubbed and kneaded into his red cheeks splashed into the air each time the leather paddles whacked him. Finally, he lowered his torso and that caused the clamps on his nipples to weigh down and pull meanly on his fleshy nubs.

"Ohhhhh f-fuckkkk..." he seethed, bucking and thrashing on the device.

"Another half hour session Mr. Stevenson," I said.

I picked up his clipboard and wheeled a chair with me out of the control booth and next to the machine he was on.

"Now Mr. Stevenson, besides being a medical doctor I sometimes dabble in psychiatry," I said to him, sitting down next to the suffering young man.

"C-congratulations," he grunted. "OWWWWWW!!!! My poor butt!"

"While you're being spanked for the fourth session I thought we would have a question and answer session as well," I said, holding my pen above his clipboard.

He simply looked at me miserably.

"It might help to take your mind off being spanked," I said suggestively.

"Yeah, if my mind were in my ass cheeks!" he replied sarcastically.

"No matter, you will answer the questions," I said. "Now, what made you decide to choose a career as a health inspector?"

"Wh-what the fuck do you care?" he asked angrily in reply.

"Just answer the question Mr. Stevenson," I said sternly.

"I-I'm very health conscious," he replied. "I believe in a healthy life style, I eat right, I exercise as much as possible. I guess I felt that being in the health industry was the right place for me. OWWWWWW!! B-but now I wonder if that was a big mistake. L-look where the fuck this inspection landed my sorry ass."

"What is your fiancée's name?" I asked him.

"L-Linda," he replied. "WH-what does she have to do with any of this?"

"Nothing, and perhaps everything," I said. "How do you think she would feel seeing you as I have you here now?"

Before replying he looked at me sheepishly, pressing his lips tightly together.

"Answer the question Mr. Stevenson," I said to him sternly, my pen poised over his notepad.

"Sh-she would probably get turned on if she saw me hooked up to your blasted machine," he blurted through clenched teeth. "Fuck, fuck, my poor, poor butt cheeks and my nipples are killing me *you bastard.*"

To try to alleviate the pain in his clamped nipples he raised his upper torso as straight out as possible, trying to lessen the pull on the clamps.

"She would be turned on seeing you this way?" I asked him, sounding genuinely surprised at the answer he'd just given me to my question.

"Yeah, she would," he said, turning to face me, smiling in his pain. "Guess you don't think I've led such a sheltered life after all huh Doc?"

I quickly scribbled some notes on his clipboard, as the

sounds of the spindles spanking his butt cheeks were the only sounds in the room.

"OWWWWWWRRR!!!" the young man bellowed and when he grew too tired to keep his upper torso straight out he leaned down again, the tit clamps pulling meanly on his nipples. "Uhhhhnnnn, gads!!"

"Why would your fiancée be aroused seeing you this way Mr. Stevenson?" I asked the inspector.

"Sh-she has a fetish for bondage in the bedroom," he gasped in reply, curling his toes back in his socks, his penis growing harder and harder behind him as he spoke. "At least once a week she ties me up to the bed in some sort of fashion."

"Does that arouse you as well?" I asked him.

"M-most of the time, yeah, it does," he said, turning his face away from me, obviously embarrassed about giving out such private aspects of his life.

"Why do you suppose she enjoys tying you up Mr. Stevenson?" I asked.

"Huhhhhnnn, maybe it's because I'm so goddamned cute," he replied sarcastically, the spindles spinning and spinning, relentlessly spanking and spanking his ass cheeks. "OWWWWWWRRR please Doc, *please.*"

"Answer the question Mr. Stevenson," I said sternly.

"She works a job where her boss is always telling her what to do, whom to call, where to send stuff," the inspector responded in between gasps. "She has no control at her job. Tying me up during sex allows her to take some control for a change."

For a few moments I watched as the young man clenched and unclenched his hands into and out of fists. He bucked helplessly up and down on the machine, trying desperately to alleviate the way the clamps were pulling on his poor nipples. The ball/vibrator in his hole buzzed insistently; tormenting him to no end I was sure. Watching him wriggle and curl his toes back in his socks sent shivers through me.

"What does she do to you while she has you tied up Mr. Stevenson?" I asked him.

"L-lots of things, mostly she just teases me like crazy, makes me wait to sh-shoot my load," he replied breathlessly. "Sort of like what the fuck you're doing to me here right now you bastard!!"

"Does she make you wait to have sex with her?" I asked him.

"Th-that is none of your business you crazy doctor," Dan Stevenson barked at me, his hands clenched tighter than tight in fists. "Let me off this thing already!!"

Smiling, I made a few more notes on his clipboard, stood up and walked back to the control room.

"I scored one there didn't I Doc?" he yelled at my back as I walked into the control room. "You didn't make me answer your question that time. I scored a winner didn't I you bastard?"

"Mr. Stevenson, I have just increased this half hour spanking session to a full hour for your refusal to answer my question," I said to him from my control booth, speaking into the microphone. "Do you wish to have it increased to two hours?"

"An, an hour???" he squealed loudly and involuntarily hoisted his upper torso, looking straight across at me. "A whole fucking hour??? *You goddamned maniac!!*"

The spindles spun and spanked him and spun and spanked him and spun and spanked him...

"I-I'll answer the question Dr. Bottoms, come on, I was just kidding," he sniveled, looking at me pleadingly.

"Oh, I know you will answer the question Mr. Stevenson," I said. "At the end of the one hour spanking session you will answer the question.

He clenched his teeth in out right rage.

"Refusal to answer the question a second time will result in a two hour spanking session," I said to him and the look of rage seemed to disappear instantly.

"So, do you still feel like you've scored a win Mr. Stevenson?" I asked him, grinning meanly at him.

"N-no Doc, actually I feel like the world's biggest loser right about now," the young man replied and lowered his upper torso.

Tears flowed from his eyes and he shook and trembled on the machine as the tit clamps again tortured and pulled on his nipples.

"Fuck," he whispered, his lips trembling as well.

At the end of the half-hour I again stepped out of the control booth. I had Dan Stevenson's snipped underpants in my hand. I sat down on the chair next to him and he watched as I took a long hearty sniff of his underpants.

"P-pervert," he grunted. "F-first you were sniffing my damned smelly socks and now you're fucking sniffing my god-damned underpants," he swore at me, bathed in sweat from head to toe now and smelling with it as well.

"Questions and answers Mr. Stevenson," I said to him and put his underpants back in my lab coat pocket. "Time once again for questions and answers."

He looked at me miserably, his sweat soaked wavy hair now hanging in his face.

"Trust me, it will make the added half hour I gave you go by a little quicker," I said, trying to sound reassuring but sounding mocking.

"O-okay man, you are in charge after all," he panted.

"Now, tell me, does your fiancee tie you up and make you wait to have sex with her?" I asked him.

He nodded his handsome head up and down vigorously.

"Y-yes, sh-she makes me wait Doc, she gets me all hard and bothered and then she makes me lie there totally erect, oozing my pre cum while she struts around the room naked," he replied, trying his best to speak coherently as he was spanked and spanked. "Sometimes she even blindfolds me while she makes me wait."

"Ah, so she won't even let you look at her while you're waiting," I said and wrote on his clipboard.

"R-right, th-that frustrates me even more and keeps me even harder," the young man grunted. "OWWWWW fuck, another goddamned half hour of this shit!!"

He bucked and squirmed miserably in the clutches of the machine, his whole muscular body awash with sweat and goose bumps.

"I must say Mr. Stevenson that I am learning quite a lot about you here today," I said, looking at him like a proud father. "I suppose I can only hope that you too are learning a lot about yourself as well."

"Y-yeah, I'm learning that I'm a goddamned asshole for having let you talk me into this fucked up situation," he barked at me.

"Now, now Mr. Stevenson, remember the two hour spanking session I warned you about," I said to him, pointing a finger at him. "Besides, you wanted this demonstration."

"I wanted a demonstration for a minute or so, not five or six hours!!" he blurted and once again he was hanging his upper torso down and sniveling uncontrollably.

When the second half-hour of his one-hour spanking session was over I was already in the control booth. I slowly turned off the spindles. He breathed a loud sigh of relief as they again stopped spanking him.

"Feeling okay out there Mr. Stevenson?" I asked him, speaking into the microphone.

"Y-yeah, j-just great," he replied, sounding weak at that point.

From a small refrigerator in the control booth I got a quart-sized bottle of mineral water. Dan Stevenson looked like he could really use the drink right about now. I didn't want him dehydrating on me after all. With the mineral water in hand I walked over to the immobilized young health inspector.

"Thirsty Mr. Stevenson?" I asked him.

Hanging there on my machine he simply nodded that he was indeed thirsty.

I took the cap off the bottle and held it to his trembling lips. He gulped down the water gratefully.

"Th-thank you, I guess," he said breathlessly after having drunk nearly half the contents of the bottle.

"You're very welcome," I said, capping the bottle and putting it down on the floor.

He moaned softly, as I stepped behind him and rubbed another goodly amount of aloe cream on his very well spanked butt cheeks.

"I must say Mr. Stevenson, you must have very sensitive skin," I said, rubbing the palm of my hand lovingly over and over his spanked cheeks. "Your butt cheeks are beyond red at this point."

"Gee, I wonder why," he muttered sarcastically.

"Yes, they're a dark shade of crimson right now," I said, kneading and rubbing the aloe thoroughly onto him, loving the feel of his heated backside under the palm of my hand.

I stole a couple of squeezes of his delectable ass cheeks, but I think he was in too much pain to really notice. Then, stepping away from him I headed back to the control room.

"Y-you're not going to spank me again so soon are you Doctor Bottoms?" the young man asked me, sounding desperate now.

"Not until I've milked you again," I said cheerfully, looking at him as I walked past him and into the control room.

"Oh geez," he whimpered and lifted his upper torso up straight.

By now his nipples had been squeezed up to the size of two pencil erasers in the tit clamps. Smiling at him through the glass I turned the dial that controlled the latex suction device on my machine. The thing came up out of the bowels of the machine and secured itself tightly around Dan Stevenson's erect penis.

"Ohhhhhhhh fuck, yeah, goddamned thing is in love with my joystick Doc," the young inspector panted and then lowered his upper torso.

I turned the dial again and the lubricated latex suction device began sliding up and down Dan Stevenson's erection, sucking him off so to speak.

"Ohhh yeah, fucking A Doc," the young man said to the floor, then bucked his body up again and craned his head as far back as possible, trying to see the thing as it sucked him. "F-fuck man, I'd like to take that sucking device home with me Doc."

"So glad you're enjoying the demonstration Mr. Stevenson," I said to him from inside the control room.

"It, it's better than being spanked, that much I'll say," he gurgled and looked straight at me. "Fuck man, I'm getting close already Doc."

He clenched his teeth in ecstasy, balled his hands into fists and at that moment I was more than glad that my office and the room we were in were soundproof.

"Arrrrhhhhhh, got me creaming like a fucking bitch in heat on a summer night Doc," the young man grunted loudly, bucking wildly on my machine like a cowboy riding a mechanical bull. "Ohhh yeah, fucking shooting my damned load man!!"

I watched as his mess erupted from him and landed with his earlier mess in the container attached to the back of the machine. Grinning fiendishly from ear to ear I put my hand on the control dial for the suction device.

"Ohhhhrrrrr fuck man, that felt great, totally fucking awesome Doc," Dan Stevenson panted, his head bobbing up and down. "Th-think I can have more water by the way?"

"Certainly, as soon as you've shot one more load for me Mr. Stevenson," I said and turned up the power on the suction device.

"S-say what?" he gibbered through his trembling lips.

Suddenly, as the suction device slid down and he thought it was about to slide off his penis it quickly snuggled up again, engulfing him tightly.

"Ohhhhrrrr fuck, *sh-shit man, no, no!!*" the young man screeched. "Shit, you're worse than a mad fucking scientist Doc! Turn the suction device off man! Don't be making it suck me right after I've just shot a hefty load. Shit, I'm all sensitive and sexy down there right now!!"

"I'll say you're sexy Mr. Stevenson," I said and turned the dial up to full power.

"Ohhh fuck, my tits are stinging man, wh-what the fuck is

up with that shit?" he barked at me, reeling uncontrollably on the machine as the suction device feasted on him.

"After a man shoots his load his nipples become extremely sensitive Mr. Stevenson," I said to him.

"Huh? I-I never noticed that before," he said, sounding totally confused.

"Perhaps it's because you've never had your nipples clamped when shooting your load in the past Mr. Stevenson," I chuckled.

"Fuck man, I'd pay anyone a hundred fucking dollars to get those clamps off my nipples Doc," the young man said loudly and in pain. "God, that suction device is really in love with my joy-stick huh? I-I'm not going to have any left for my fiancee tonight when I get home."

He panted, sweaty and grunting as he hung on the machine like a side of beef in a butcher's freezer.

"Huuuhhhhnnn, goddamned thing is nibbling my slit Doc," he gasped. "Fuck, but that drives me crazy man!!"

Stepping out of the control room again I made my way over to my prize young man and the machine. I stepped behind him and jiggled the ball/vibrator in his hole.

"Ayyyyyhhhhhrrrrr, f-fuck, WH-what are you doing back there Doc?" Dan Stevenson squealed.

"Just about to make an adjustment Mr. Stevenson," I said and in a quick pull yanked the ball/vibrator out of his hole.

I quickly undid the thin wires attached to the ball/vibrator around his peach fuzzed balls.

"Ohhhhhhhhh ohhhhhhhh fuck," he gasped breathlessly, his rosebud hole twitching, missing the device already.

His hole was sweaty and moist, seeing as I'd left the ball/vibrator in there for quite some time.

"One finger deep inside you should do it I would think Mr. Stevenson," I said cheerfully.

"O-one finger?" he asked, squirming like a fish out of water. "And what the fuck does that mean?"

I watched as the latex sheath worked him and then all at

once slid my right-handed index finger deep into the crevice that was his warm ass hole.

"Ohhhhh shhhhiiiittt, I-I'm going to cum you pervert, shit, that did it is right!!" he screamed nearly insanely.

I quickly extracted my finger from his hole and as he shot his third load I made my way back to the control room. After he was done shooting his load this time I would give him some water and then it was to be spanking time again for the young man...

"Ayyyyyrrrrr I, I swear, I n-never shot my load so soon after just getting off," he screamed, looking at me in the control room.

Once again his mess of creamy sperm erupted from his slit and was deposited in the small container on the back of the machine. The suction device worked tirelessly at extracting every possible drop from the young man as he bucked and swore, hanging on the machine.

"Ohhhhhhhhh man, what a sensation," he panted.

Suddenly, he hoisted his upper torso straight out again, his hands splayed wide open at his sides and his mouth curled wide open, his eyes squeezed shut.

"Ooooooooooo f-fuck, my, my poor goddamned nipples you crazy doctor," he bellowed, swinging his torso from side to side, trying unsuccessfully to get the stinging nipple clamps off himself.

I chuckled meanly in the control room, watching as the young man suffered...

When he was finally done I turned the control dial for the suction device and it slid off his softening penis.

"Ohhhhhhh," he whispered, his head hanging down, sweat dripping from his hair and forehead.

The suction device disappeared back down into the bowels of the machine and I stepped out of the control room with the half full bottle of mineral water... The young man once again gratefully gulped down the water, his lips trembling around the bottle as he drank.

"D-Doc, how about letting me off this machine of yours?" he asked me beseechingly when he was done drinking, having finished what was left of the water. "Th-the demonstration was a total success I would say. Wouldn't you agree?"

"Now, now Mr. Stevenson, you still have a way to go," I said to him, wagging a finger in his handsome face. "I wouldn't want you to feel cheated and go back to your superiors and give them a less than glowing report on my facility."

I tucked the empty mineral water bottle under my arm, stepped in front of the young man and reached under his hanging torso to his nipples. I unhooked the clamps and took them off his nipples.

"Ayyyyyrrrrrrrrr ohhhhhhhh shhhiiiitttt!!!!" he screamed like a banshee.

"Feels worse now that they're off eh Mr. Stevenson?" I asked him, holding up the tit clamps.

"Ohhhhhhh fuck, wh-why is that Doc?" he garbled.

"It's the blood rushing back into your numbed nipples," I explained. "You'll be fine in a few minutes."

I stepped away from him and walked back toward the control room.

"Or then again, maybe you won't be," I chuckled.

In the control room I slowly turned the dial that controlled the spanking spindles.

"Ohhhhhhh no, no, not again," the inspector grumbled miserably.

The sounds of his exquisite ass cheeks being spanked were music to my ears. Smiling meanly from ear to ear I turned the power up to highest capacity.

"Ayyyyyrrrrrr shhhitttt," he grunted in a high crescendo.

I sat and watched from the control room for a few minutes as the young man was spanked at top speed by the leather paddles on the revolving spindles. I made some more notes on his clipboard then took a black silk blindfold from the same drawer I had gotten the tit clamps from.

"Wh-why are you blindfolding me Doc?" the young man asked, sounding terrified as I stood in front of him a few seconds later, tying the silk cloth over his eyes. "OWWWWW, fucking things spanking the tar out of me!!"

"Well, when you told me that your fiancé blindfolds you every once in a while and makes you wait to have sex with her I thought that this may remind you of that," I said mockingly, knotting the cloth in the back of his head. "And while you're here having your demonstration of my machine I'm going to have to go and make some rounds in the facility. I do have patients and students to check on after all."

"WH-what???" he blurted, looking around stupidly with his blindfolded eyes. "Y-you mean you're leaving me alone here man? Y-you can't!!"

"Only for a half hour or so," I said to him reassuringly, jiggling the knot in his blindfold. "When I get back I'll see about milking another good load of sperm from you."

"No, no Doc, please man, don't leave me here like this," he begged as I left the room, stepping into my office.

I closed the door behind me and walked over to the video tape recorder that was mounted on the wall between my office and the room that Dan Stevenson was in. I double-checked to make sure it was working properly. It was. Two tapes were being recorded of the young man as he was spanked and milked on my machine. One tape for was me and for my growing collection and one tape for the young man to insure his silence where my machine and this experience were concerned. The videotape also insured that he would be back in the future for another demonstration, should I decide that I would want to work him again on my machine. Smiling, I sat down behind my desk and picked up the phone, dialing a number.

"Global Inspections," the young man on the other end said after picking up the phone. "This is Mike Aldana, how can I help you?"

"Hello Mr. Aldana, this is Doctor Bottoms, how are you today?" I asked the handsome young man, smiling meanly from ear to ear.

I heard Mike Aldana gulp hard at the sound of my voice.

"D-Doctor Bottoms, er, how are you Sir?" Mike Aldana

asked me, feigning pleasantries.

"Oh, I'm doing fine Mike, just fine," I said, taking Dan Stevenson's underpants from my lab pocket. "I was thinking we should set up an appointment. It's been a while since you've seen my machine demonstrated."

"Is, is that really necessary Sir?" he asked me, sounding miserable. "Last time I was there I got hours worth of a demonstration."

"Very necessary," I said sternly. "One of your colleagues is almost done now as we speak. I could more than likely fit you in today, early evening shall we say?"

The young man said "Yes Sir" and hung up the phone. Leaning back in my chair I laughed hysterically and sniffed Dan Stevenson's underpants…

A Boner Book

From Out of the Woods

I was driving home from upstate New York about a month ago when this happened. Since it happened I haven't stopped thinking about it and I suppose that's why I decided to finally write about it. It was about three AM on a Saturday morning and I was returning home from a week's business trip. My name is David Stevens. I work as a salesman for a jewelry corporation. I was actually supposed to be headed home on Sunday but after all the work I had done I could not wait for the comforts of my own apartment. Dressed in a blue pinstriped suit, white shirt, burgundy silk necktie and black lace-up wingtips I drove at the required speed limit toward Manhattan, humming along to the jazz song playing on the radio. On the sides of me were nothing but woods, dense woods, for miles and miles and as far as the eye could see. Suddenly, from out of the woods on my right side I saw a man come running out into the road. At first I thought I had worked too hard all week and that my eyes were deceiving me. He was dressed in only a pair of white briefs and filthy white calf length sweat socks. As he ran out in front of my oncoming car, waving his arms in the air, I instantly slammed on the brakes.

"SHIT!!!" I roared as the car came to a grinding and screeching halt.

He was standing there in front of my car, his palms resting on the hood. He was fairly tall. He had a neatly trimmed beard, a thin mustache, thick black curly hair that reached just about to his shoulders, piercing blue eyes and a hairy chest. Muscles rippled all over him and his body was shining and glistening with sweat in the moonlight and the headlights of my car. He waved at me, ran to the passenger side window of my car, (which was rolled down) and leaned his head and shoulders in.

"P-please Mister, please help me," he said breathlessly, the scent of his sweat filling the small interior of my vehicle. "If those two catch me they'll want more…and I can't, I just can't possibly take anymore…God, I'm so sore…"

"Just exactly what seems to be the problem bud?" I asked him, as droplets of sweat dripped off him, landing on the passenger seat of my car. "What in Sam hell are you doing running around out here in just your under shorts and socks?"

"I-I'll explain it all," he said just as breathlessly. "But please, please give me a ride to a police station or something…I swear to you Mister…if those two catch me…"

"I know, they'll want more and you can't possibly take anymore," I finished for him.

"Yeah, so please…GOD, I'm so sore…" he pleaded.

Suddenly, two big and burly looking men emerged from out of the woods.

"There he is Cleeve!!" one of the men yelled. "Let's get him!!"

"Mister, please, open the door!!" the man yelled at me desperately as he tried to reach down to undo the latch on the car door, but the window being rolled down only part of the way inhibited his reach.

When I saw the two men running toward my car I quickly reached over, unlatched the door and shoved it open as the man pulled his head and shoulders from the window.

The man in just his under shorts and socks literally jumped into the passenger seat. As he locked the door I put my foot on the gas pedal.

"HEY!!! HEY!!! You mother-fucker, he's ours!!!" I heard one of the two men outside the car yelling as I drove off with my terrified and trembling passenger.

As I drove the man now sitting next to me placed his face in his hands and sobbed, shaking uncontrollably.

"God, oh God," he whimpered. "Fucking bastards…"

I reached over and placed a hand on his head as he crouched down in the seat, running my fingers in his silky long black curly hair. I hadn't realized just how very beautiful he really was…in a very exotic sort of way actually. I loved the feel of his hair in my fingers.

"You okay bud?" I asked him, twining his hair in my fingers.

"I-I will be…eventually…" he said through his tears. "Thank you for picking me up."

"It uh, it's okay…you really didn't give me too much of a choice you know," I said, giving the back of his sweat soaked neck a gentle squeeze.

After a few minutes he sat up and wiped the tears off his face.

"Feeling any better?" I asked him.

"Yeah, now I am," he replied.

"Uh, look, my name is David, David Stevens," I said to him. "Would you care to tell me what's going on and why you were out in the woods in just your under shorts and socks?"

"Sure," he said. "I guess you are entitled to an explanation after all. My name is Victor Burton. I'm a writer and I had come out here camping and to do some writing by myself, get in touch with nature and all that shit…"

"Uh-huh…" I said as I drove.

"I was at my campsite minding my own damned business," he said angrily. "Suddenly those two bastards you saw back there showed up out of nowhere and ambushed me. The fuckers, they worked me over for a good while…a long while. One of them held my arms behind me while the other one slammed punches into my gut, beat my thighs and legs with a long fallen tree branch, and pummeled my gut some more, really knocking the wind and fight out of me. He slapped my face over and over till I was nearly unconscious. Then they stripped me to my briefs and socks and worked me over some more. GOD!! That was totally humiliating, being forcibly stripped like that, but it got worse Mr. Stevens, it got worse. They fucking tied me to a tree and then, then…"

His voice filled with emotion and I could tell that he was about to lose it again. I stopped the car on the side of the deserted road directly under a lamppost. The light from the lamppost illuminated his body, making him look even more exotic. He was muscularly curved and proportioned beautifully. I thought how he could have been a model for the "International Male" catalogue. His head was leaned back against the headrest on the seat and he was looking straight up at the ceiling of the car. I reached over and with the tips of my fingers I gently touched his beard, pulling on it just a little.

"What did they do to you Victor?" I asked him. "Did they rob you?"

He took a deep breath which caused his chest to heave nice and big. His nipples looked so delicious, two brown nubs sticking out of his black chest hair, very pronounced and eraser-like nubs to be exact.

"Worse than robbed me man..." he said slowly as I continued fingering his beard, loving the prickly feel of it between my fingers. "They, they, they..."

"They fucking milked me like crazy man!!" he spat angrily. "Fuckers tied me up to a tree and sucked load after load of sperm out of me till I thought I would bleed from my piss hole. Then they tortured my poor balls, squeezed the bejesus out of them, twisted them like they were bottle caps, and tongued them hard, real fucking hard till they were swollen beyond reason. Fucking tree bark was cutting into my back but they didn't give a rat's ass. They were having too much fun injecting Viagra into me and torturing the fuck out of me...every fifteen minutes or so they milked me when I was able to get hard again. Fuckers injected me...with Viagra... Do I look like I need Viagra Mr. Stevens???"

"They sucked your cock Victor?" I asked him, looking at his crotch now.

"Over and over man..." he sputtered, still looking at his crotch, him not realizing that I too was now transfixed on the huge package I saw there between his long sexy muscular legs. "That shit can start to be painful after a while...even if you've been given an aid like Viagra...and especially if your family jewels are being tortured...SHIT!!!"

"I bet it could," I said softly, reluctantly taking my eyes from his crotch.

He looked at me with tear-filled eyes.

"How did you get away from them if you were all tied up?" I asked him.

"They had untied me from the tree because they said it was now their turn," Victor replied. "They were going to fuck my ass man. *Can you believe that shit???* Well, as soon as I was untied I ran, man did I fucking run, faster than the six million dollar man, remember him?"

"And that's when I found you?" I asked him.

"Yeah, that's when you found me," he said. "Or maybe I found you, however you want to see it. I had been running like crazy through the woods."

"Victor, I have some clothes in the trunk," I said to him. "I don't know if they'll fit you but you sure as shit can't show up in a police or trooper station in just your under shorts and socks."

"I-I guess you're right Mr. Stevens," he said.

The way he had called me Mr. Stevens sent a chill up my spine and at that moment I knew what I wanted from this beautiful and exotic looking man. I figured that if the guy's who had captured him in the woods had given him Viagra he was probably still potent. Before the night was over his cock was going to be milked a few more times. No doubt he would be a tad sorer but he looked strong enough to deal with it.

"Let's go and have a look and see if we can find something that will fit you," I said.

We got out of the car and into the warm sultry night. We walked to the back of my car and stood facing each other. A few times Victor's eyes darted around, no doubt thinking that his two captors would somehow appear to encapsulate him yet again. I took a deep breath, squatted in front of him, and unceremoniously buried my face against Victor's sweat scented under shorts.

"OH God no...no Mr. Stevens..." Victor panted.

I rubbed my tongue over his sticky under shorts, savoring the smell and taste of his exquisite sweat. I even smelled the remnants of his piss and cum in there. I grabbed his legs in a tight grip and moved him to the car.

"OH GOD..." he whimpered breathlessly.

In moments Victor was sitting up on the back trunk of my car, his legs spread wide, his cock out of his briefs and in my mouth. His manhood was long and fat, a real knockwurst if ever there was one. I was able to see why the two guys who had captured him had had a grand old time milking him like a steer. He leaned back on his elbows and watched intently as I sucked his big sore cock.

"Ohhhhhh..." he moaned in a mixture of ecstasy and agony. *"What a night this has been..."*

I ran the palms of my hands over his long shapely legs and down to his calves, loving how the muscles in his legs felt. I snapped the elastic in his sweat socks against his calves a few times and continued sucking his giant meat. His cock was delicious and throbbing like crazy in my mouth. I knew that with the way he had been dosed with the Viagra that his cock was capable of shooting off more than a few more loads. And it would I decided...no need to waste his good stuff...then I would drive him to the police station.

"Oh God Mr. Stevens, I'm getting close now," Victor said breathlessly.

He shot his load and squirted a small amount of white creamy jazz into my mouth.

"Oh yeah!! Yeah!!" he panted wildly and rocked on the car. "Oh man, at least I wasn't tied up that time."

A light came on in my head as his cock slipped slowly from between my lips. I helped him off the car to his socked feet. He stood docile as I proceeded to slurp one of his pointy nipples into my mouth.

"Oh fuck..." he moaned up at the sky. *"What a night this has been..."*

Victor placed his hands up behind his head and gyrated his sexy curved body seductively as I chewed, sucked and kissed his nipple like crazy.

"OHHHHH..." he groaned then. "Never been worked on like this before...and so much in one fucking night. Bastards gave me Viagra...I'm so horned up..."

I moved to his other nipple and worked that one the same way as I had the first one. Victor ran his hands through my hair and squeezed my ears as I went on feasting on his nub. When I stopped Victor's nipples were erect, red, and somewhat swollen. I looked at him and ran a hand over his hairy chest.

"Now let's see what I have in here for you," I said, taking my keys out of my suit jacket pocket.

I opened the trunk of my car. In the trunk was a piece of luggage which contained all my clothes from my business trip, a spare tire, and a pile of rope. I picked out a good length of rope and held it up in front of the underwear clad man.

"Oh no Mr. Stevens, please no..." Victor whimpered and took a few steps back.

"If you run Victor you may wind up back with those two guys again," I said to him, approaching him with the rope. "I won't hurt you, I promise you that. I just want to have a little fun with you. Then, and only then will I take you to safety."

I stepped close to him and realized what a prick I was being. I mean, the poor fucker was standing there trembling in his under shorts and socks, but he was so fucking hot that I couldn't seem to stop myself. I wanted to see how he would look all roped up. I ran my fingertips over his beard and mustache. His tongue darted out of his mouth and he licked my fingers.

"You truly are the most beautiful fucking thing I have ever seen Victor," I said breathlessly. "Now, arms up behind you..."

Victor did as he was told, crossing his arms over each other behind himself. He stood still as I roped his arms tightly together in three places.

"What a night this has been..." he said for the third time.

I took more rope out of the trunk and roped up Victor's upper body, leaving his nipples visible for my use. When I was done tying him I closed the trunk of the car, sat him up on it again, and leaned down.

"Oh God, and here we go again," Victor moaned as I sucked his cock into my mouth a second time.

Victor reeled and moaned about how sore his poor cock was as I sucked him slowly to a new hard-on. I sucked the guy's erection like crazy and I'm not ashamed to say that it tasted magnificent as it stuck out of the fly opening of his under shorts, all sticky and musty like. I would let his cock go soft in my mouth just to tease him and just so I could suck him back up again to a hard pillar of man-meat. He looked beyond hot and sexy all roped up with his sweat soaked muscular body shining in the glow of the lamppost. It took a while but finally he shot his load again…right into my mouth. I wondered how much Viagra his two captors had given him earlier.

"OHHHHH GOD, yeah!!!" Victor cried out loudly, looking up at the night sky. "FUCK yeah!!!"

I continued sucking his cock even after it had gone completely soft. It felt that good in my mouth, and as pointed out, it tasted magnificent. Victor reeled in a state of fury as I sucked him some more, him begging me to stop at that point. I could not get enough of his beautiful cock. I could tell now why those two guys who'd captured him wanted to milk the tar out of him and then some. There was just something magical about the exotic guy's sperm. When I was done I again helped him off the car and to his feet. He stood in front of me as I squeezed his nipple.

"What is it about you Victor?" I asked him. "I can't get enough of you…"

I squeezed his nipples harder yet, inflicting mild pain.

"OHHHHHH my tits…" Victor whimpered. "Please Mr. Stevens…"

I kissed him on the lips and told him that I wanted to lick his hole. Without being told to he turned around and slumped his body on the car. I peeled his under shorts down in the back and tucked them under his thighs, revealing two of the sexiest and coconut shaped ass globes I had ever seen. His hole was small, pink and ready for some serious licking. I plunged my tongue into his gaping crevice and began eating it like mad. He tasted raw and stinky, a real sweaty hole the exotic looking guy had. He groaned and grunted in a man's passion as I ate his ass. Victor howled like a trapped animal but in ecstasy at the same time. He said "Mr. Stevens" over and over breathlessly. When his hole was good and sopped with my saliva I stuck a finger in it and he thrashed on the car, moaning loudly.

"Never been fucked in the ass eh Victor?" I asked him as I slowly retracted my finger from his chute.

"N-no Mr. Stevens," he replied as I stood up straight behind him. "But I get the feeling I'm about to be..."

I took my rigidly hard cock out of my suit pants and positioned myself behind him. Slowly, I inserted my pole into Victor's wet hole. He moaned in pain a little but then contentment as I thrust a little at a time into his sweet crevice. His ass lips seemed to be sucking my cock into him. When half my cock was in his hole he begged me to slide it all the way in. I held him by his hips and did just that. I fucked the guy like crazy, slowly, and fast. Victor cried out in delight as he lost his rectal virginity, grunting about how he never knew how very good it could feel to be fucked in the ass. When I could not hold back anymore I shot a giant load into Victor's hole. My juices flooded him, my hot steaming cum causing him to reel even more. When I was spent my cock slipped out of him. I yanked the beautiful guy to a standing position and held him close to me as he panted for breath. His roped up body felt great in my arms and I stroked his fine-looking hair.

"Oh God, *what a night this has been...*" Victor said again and I smiled, thinking of just how much this beautifully striking man had been used and abused this night.

Moments passed and I released my hold on him. I held him out in front of myself by his upper arms, looking at him, drinking in the sight of him, this beautiful and exotic looking man. He was utterly magnificent, breathtaking; a poet could write millions of verses just about his smile. What a sight he was to behold. I looked down at his cock as it stuck out of his under shorts and took a deep breath.

"I want it again Victor," I whispered.

"Oh God no Mr. Stevens," Victor panted. "I-I couldn't possibly…"

"Maybe this way you can," I said, took my tie off and tied it over Victor's eyes, effectively blindfolding him.

"*Oh shit…*" he whispered.

I got more rope out of the trunk and tied his feet, his knees and his thighs. I loved the control I had exacted over this exotic creature that was called a man on Viagra. I slammed the trunk of the car closed and Victor shook and tottered, awkwardly balanced as I gobbled his cock into my mouth a third time.

"OHHHHHHH FUCCCKKK…" he moaned in exhaustion.

After forcing another Viagra induced small load out of him I untied the poor guy, took the blindfold off him, and re-knotted my tie around my neck. Victor stood there panting, looking at me gratefully.

"Feeling good?" I asked him.

"More than good Mr. Stevens," he said happily. "I feel great…drained…but great…"

Victor pulled his under shorts up in the back and packed his cock into them in the front.

"Now, let's see about those clothes for you…finally…" I said and squeezed his shoulder.

I turned around to open the trunk. Suddenly Victor yelled out, "Mr. Stevens!!" but it was too late. I was clocked on the head from behind and fell to the ground in a stupor.

"Mr. Stevens help me!!" I heard Victor screaming.

On the ground I managed to open my eyes only halfway. I saw the two men who had chased Victor out of the woods earlier. They had Victor by his arms and legs and they were carrying him away, back into the woods.

"*Mr. Stevens, oh God!!!*" Victor screamed helplessly.

I blacked out.

When I came to a while later there was no sign of Victor anywhere. On the side of the road however I saw the exotic guy's under shorts. The bastards had taken them off him. I stood up, let the dizziness pass as I rubbed the spot on my head where I'd been bopped and trotted over to where the under shorts were lying on the ground. I picked them up and saw that there was a small piece of paper pinned to the inside of them. I unhitched the paper from the under shorts, unfolded it, and read what was written on it. The note read, "He's ours you fuck and always will be. C&O" I screamed Victor's name over and over but received no reply, only the sound of my voice in desperation echoing back to me. I put the under shorts in my suit jacket pocket and walked dejectedly to my car. I knew that in my sexual urges I had let the guy down, the poor fucking guy...

It's now been more than a month since that business trip and my roadside encounter with the beautiful and exotic man named Victor. I never found out what became of him. I told the police about him and how he was viciously abducted by two men. I tried my best to remember and describe them but nothing came from that either. The cop who took my statement said it sounded like the work of Cleeve and Otis. I had no idea who Cleeve and Otis were, nor what the cop was talking about when he said that it sounded like their work. For all I know Victor is *still* in the clutches of those two burly men, being milked and fucked for their perverted pleasures. The only reminder I have of Victor is a pair of his white under shorts, which I will keep forever or until a miracle causes me to see him again...and I can place the under shorts on him.

Breaking Up Is "Hard" To Do

My name is Paul Rogan. I want to tell you about the most depressing night of my life, which then turned into the kinkiest night of my life. It happened about seven months ago. Till this day I still wonder if I dealt it all, it was pretty amazing. I had been dating Linda for close to a year when on that particular night she decided to tell me that she didn't want to go out with me anymore. She wanted to date other men. She wanted to feel free again. Needless to say I was crushed. My heart was broken. Linda was the girl I thought I was going to marry. I had been so sure of it. We had met at a dinner party given by a mutual friend of ours and from the moment our eyes met I knew she was the one…or at least I thought she was. We were both young, (I'm twenty two) college graduates, energetic and hard working. I work for a bank in Manhattan as a computer systems analyst. We both enjoyed the same types of movies, music, and even Broadway shows. We began dating the night after the dinner party and it just seemed like everything in my life was perfect. Wrong, because as I said about eleven months later Linda decided to end our relationship. It was a warm September night and I drove around aimlessly after she had broken the news to me. It was after eleven o'clock at night. I thought about going to the twenty-four hour gym for a good hard workout to relieve whatever it was I was feeling (I workout four times a week and my body is really pumped up and muscular because of it) but really wasn't in the mood for working out at that moment. As I drove I realized that I had come to the street just before the boardwalk of Manhattan Beach in Brooklyn New York. I parked my car, got out, and walked to the boardwalk. I sat down on a bench and breathed heavily, tears in my eyes. I missed Linda already. As I sat there alone I listened to the sound of the waves of the ocean down on the beach. Whenever I'm feeling down or depressed I swim. It seems to relieve the ill feeling…sort of like working out does. I looked around to make sure no one was around and decided to take a swim. I took off my sneakers and sweat socks and holding them in hand I walked barefoot down to the beach. When I was a few feet from where the waves ended and broke on the sand I stripped down to my white briefs, piling my clothes up on the sand, laying my sneakers atop them to weigh them down in case of wind. The cool air caressed my muscular body and I was feeling better already. Slowly, I walked into the cold water of the ocean. It welcomed me like the arms of a lover. When I was up to my chest I leaned forward and swam out further.

"AHHHHH…" I sighed. "Feels great…"

The cold water invigorated me, caressed me, and made my nine inch cock hard as a rock in my briefs. I swam back and forth, trying not to think of Linda. As I was floating on my back, the moon shining down on me, I glanced at the beach and saw two guys sitting down on the sand. They lit cigarettes and seemed to be just relaxing. I was worried for a moment that they were homeless and would steal my clothes. My wallet and car keys were in my pants after all. The thought of having to report a robbery in just my wet briefs was not too thrilling. But the two guys just seemed to be minding their business, not bothering any of my stuff. A short while later I swam for shore. I was totally exhausted but feeling good and invigorated. I walked on the sand to where my clothes were and decided to lay down for a few minutes before getting dressed to head on home. I lay down and the white sugary sand stuck to the backs of my tree trunks like legs and muscular back. I would have to swim again to rinse off before getting into my clothes. I closed my eyes and relaxed, not thinking of Linda…and not thinking of the two guys who were now silently making their way over to me. My cock was still hard as a rock in my briefs. Actually, my cock is hard more often than it is not. As the cool breeze caressed me I suddenly felt it. My nipples were being sucked! My eyes shot open and I could not believe what I was seeing…and feeling. The two guys who I had seen earlier were stretched out on my sides, each of them sucking one of my big nipples, their arms then folded over my arms, holding me down on the sand. It had all happened so damned fast.

"H-hey…WH-what the fuck do you think you're doing???" I grunted, lifting my head up off the sand and looking down at them in disbelief as they sucked, licked, kissed and teased my nipples with the tips of their tongues. "OHHHHHH shit, that feels fucking awesome dudes…"

"Just relax…dude…" one of the guys said and gave my big succulent balls a squeeze through my sopping wet briefs.

He then resumed working my nipple. They ran their hands over my big rock hard chest, and ran their fingertips over the impression of my hard cock in my briefs as they continued working the fuck out of my nipples.

"OHHHHHHH fuck…" I moaned my head still lifted up off the sand. "I ain't a faggot you guys but I got to admit that that sure does feel great…fucking fuckers, working my big tits…YEAH!"

I lowered my head back down on the sand and looked up at the moon. Goose bumps broke out all over my body as the two guys went on working my nipples. In no time my nipples were erect and fucking hard. The two guys ran their tongues gently over them, running the palms of their hands over and under my huge male cleavage, my giant pecs. I saw that they were both dressed in bathing suits. I guessed that they had come out for some night swimming and found me as a bonus of sorts.

"OHHHHHH…" I moaned. "You two are driving me crazy…"

They slurped my nipples back into their mouths and gave them another good workout with their tongues. After a while my nipples were feeling a little sore but the two guys still chowed down on them. The mixture of pleasure and slight pain was totally invigorating…it was more than invigorating actually, it was fucking awesome! They had taken their folded arms off my arms, knowing by then that I wasn't going to try anything. Hell, why would I try to stop them or run off? What they were doing to me felt great. Linda had never gone near my nipples in all our time together. This was like a whole new experience for me. I crossed my hands up behind my head and watched as the two guys delighted in servicing my nipples.

"My name is Paul..." I said softly.

They didn't reply by telling me their names...they just went on working my nipples.

"ARRRRHHHH yeah!!" I grunted and arched my back up off the sand. "FUCKIN' A!!!"

Then, one of the guys stopped working my nipple that he had in his mouth and moved his tongue over one of my hairy armpits.

"OHHHHH shit, what's this???" I asked breathlessly. "Fucking sleazy bastard licking my armpit..."

As he worked my armpit his buddy continued working one of my nipples with his mouth and the other one with his thumb and first finger, squeezing it, twisting it, and pinching it.

"OHHHHH yeah, fucking guys are making me batty," I groaned. "My goddamned girlfriend never worked on me like this..."

They stopped what they were doing for a second, looked at each other across my prone muscular body, smiled, and quickly resumed working on my nipples and armpits. The other guy moved to my other armpit and then they were licking, sucking, and kissing my armpits. My nipples had been sucked up past erect. They were as pointy as bullets and feeling just as hard. Goose bumps were all over me, I was sweating in the cool breeze, and my cock... GOD...my cock was harder than it had ever been before. It throbbed like crazy in my wet briefs, hard as a fucking rock, and oozing and oozing my pre seed like I can't begin to tell you. After a while they stopped working my armpits and I watched breathlessly as they moved toward my crotch.

"OHHHH yeah, go for it you sleazy fuckers," I gasped when I saw they were a tad reluctant to go near my hard man-hood. "Suck my cock..."

They didn't need to be told twice. They reached into the fly opening of my white briefs and pulled out my hard, fat and throbbing sausage-sized cock, along with my big hairy balls. They looked at each other in awe, marveling at the size and girth of my huge meat. They each licked the tip of it a few times like it was an ice cream cone and then they took turns sucking it, pulling it deep into their mouths, and running their lips and tongue over the sides of it. They tongued my big balls, applying pressure to them, driving me wild, and making my head spin.

"OHHHHHH GOD!!!" I roared and my voice echoed across the deserted beach. "Fuckers..."

Then, as one of them sucked my meat the other one ran his tongue all over my balls at the same time. He pulled my balls alternately into his mouth and sucked them with real gusto. I sat up on my elbows and watched in awe as the two guys sucked my cock and lapped my balls.

"OH GAWD, this is fucking unbelievable," I grunted.

As I sat there in my briefs having my cock and balls worked on I ran one hand over my chest and squeezed one of my nipples. It felt hard and leathery between my fingers...from the workout my two new buddies had given it beforehand. When I felt myself getting close to shooting my load I laid back down on the sand, my muscular arms at my sides.

"Oh yeah you cock hungry fuckers..." I moaned breathlessly. "Getting close now...oh yeah get ready you guys..."

The guy who had my cock in his mouth at that moment took it out, grabbed it tightly in his hand, and held it as I shot my big creamy load...all over my chest, my stomach, and onto my nipples.

"OHHHHH yeah, yeah!!! FUCKING A you guys, fucking A!!" I roared as I shot globs of hot velvety jazz all over me. Fuckers, milking the tar outa me...FUCK!!!"

I bucked and writhed on the sand in sheer ecstasy as one of the guys held my cock and the other one continued licking at my balls...hard. When I was done and they had squeezed every possible drop of cum out of me I sat up on my elbows and watched as they eagerly licked my cum off my chest and stomach, sucking it off my now very sensitive nipples also. I moaned and groaned in a man's passion as they licked me like I was an ice cream cone.

"Oh yeah you two," I whispered. "Fucking turned the worst night of my life into the best night of my life."

At that moment I had completely forgotten Linda. A few minutes later I was on my knees in front of the two men, alternately sucking their cocks. Their bathing suits were down around their ankles on the sand as I, for the first time in all my life, sucked cock. I licked their pre seed off their piss slits as they pressed their hard throbbing cocks together in front of my lips. Fucking fuck, like I said, I had never sucked a man's cock before in my life, but, at that moment I was getting a damned good education in the art of it. My cock, still sticking out of my wet briefs along with my big gushy balls was again hard and throbbing, wanting to shoot another load. Can you believe that shit? And I had just cum not all that long ago. I ran my hands over the two men's legs, squeezed their thighs, and licked their balls as they stood over me, moaning and groaning in the moonlight. They squeezed each other's nipples and slapped each other's pecs as I went on alternately sucking their cocks, slurping on them, deep throating them one at a time. Every time they pressed their cocks together and held them to my lips I nibbled erotically at their slits and cock-heads. They reached down and caressed the back of my neck as I sucked and sucked them, sliding my mouth further over their cocks as I sucked. A few minutes later the first guy announced breathlessly that he was cumming and he erupted like a goddamned volcano, holding his hard cock in his hand, stroking himself all over my chest.

"OHHHHHHH yeah!!!" he crooned loudly as I leaned back in the sand and his cum landed all over my torso, stomach and nipples.

His friend wasn't too far behind. He shot his load a few seconds later, shooting a load just as big and creamy all over me. He moaned loudly in passion beside his buddy as he came and came also. As their cum dripped all over my chest, nipples and stomach I knew what without a guess I was in for next. When they were spent I laid back down on the sand without a word. I sat up on my elbows as they went to work licking their cum slowly off my chest, again slurping on my nipples like crazy, torturing them erotically at that point.

"OHHHHH you fucking guys…" I grunted and looked up at the moonlit sky. "Looks like I'm your cum buffet."

I ground my fingers into the sand as their tongues explored my huge chest, my pecs, my stomach, and of course my nipples. Damn, but those guys loved my nipples. It was as if they couldn't get enough of them. My head spinning again I laid back down on the sand. The two guys stretched out at my sides and continued slurping on me.

"I can feast on this fucking guy all night…" one of them whispered breathlessly.

I decided to do just that, to let them feast on me all they wanted. When they started taking turns poking the tips of their tongues into my belly button I cried out in a passion I never knew before. Not to mention that I'm ticklish as hell around my belly button. When they moved down to my feet I watched as they each took one of my big feet into their hands and sucked my toes one at a time. I sat up again and this time grabbed my cock in my hand. I stroked myself slowly as they sucked my toes and massaged my feet. I was swooning and sweating in an ecstasy all new to me.

"OHHHHH yeah, look at you two sleazy fuckers sucking my damned toes…" I said softly and felt myself cumming a second time as I milked my cock. "OHHHHHHHH yeah, yeah, you fuckers…feels great…"

I shot my load all over myself again and fell back on the sand on my back, panting for breath as the two guys went on and on sucking my toes. I ran my fingers through my cum all over my chest and new goose bumps broke out all over me as I squeezed my nipples. A short while later the two guys helped me to my feet and we all stood in a circle.

"Hot guy you are," one of them said to me and squeezed

one of my nipples as I packed my cock and balls into my briefs.

"Let's all take a swim and then come back for some more," the other guy said.

"You two go ahead," I said. "I'll wait here for you two to get back..."

"Come on Dude, a swim will invigorate you and do you good," the first guy said.

Before I realized what he was about to do he scooped me up off the sand and slung me across his broad shoulders.

"UFFFFFF...strong fucker you are..." I said. "Okay, a swim it is then..."

He lugged me to the ocean followed by his friend and when we were out in pretty deep water he dropped me. I landed in the water with a big splash. He swam under me and came up with me sitting atop his shoulders.

"WHOA!!!" I cried out with a big smile on my face, quickly balancing myself as he lifted me high above the water.

We rough-housed for a while in the water and they took turns hoisting me and throwing me into the water. At one point they held me afloat by my arms and sucked on my salt water tasting nipples. When we had swam enough they carried me across their shoulders back to our spot on the beach. For the next couple of hours I lay there as they sucked my cock, my nipples, and feasted on every part of me again and again. I sucked them off again and by the time we were all spent it was nearly morning. I fell asleep on the sand as they walked off without a word...

When I woke up the sun was just coming up. I stood on the sand and scanned the area for my two nameless sex buddies. They were nowhere in sight... As my cock churned in my briefs I got dressed and slowly walked up to the boardwalk and to my car. I never saw them again but I will never forget that night on the beach...

Security Guard Abduction (Jack)

"You know man, this is a lousy and fucked up thing you've done," he panted and swore through clenched teeth, sweating like crazy. "Robbing the damned store was bad enough, terrorizing those innocent people was worse, but kidnapping me was totally not called for man! Fucking kidnapping my ass, roping me the fuck up like this to this damned pole...none of it necessary dude...and now you pervert, *you goddamned degenerate,* sucking the fuck out of my big cock!! OHHHHHHHH, GOD, n-never thought I would be begging someone to stop sucking my big meat stick!!"

I never thought I would hear some big, hunky and handsome stud of a guy begging me to stop sucking him either. But seeing as I had already sucked, squeezed and pumped three big creamy loads out of him I was sure he was good for more. I was also sure that his huge cock and gamey balls were feeling pretty sore at that point. He moaned and groaned and grunted in totally macho sounding man misery as I knelt in front of him, sucking and sucking his big sausage sized meat stick like crazy. It was of the gargantuan size and irresistible I might add. I drooled madly and lustfully around it as it filled my craw, his big balls hanging down against my chin, nice and low and sweaty scented as I teased them with my fingertips. Ha, teased them and more, I fucking squeezed the bejesus out of them just for the fuck of it. Every time I squeezed his balls his hard cock twitched in my mouth. His muscular body strained and twisted beautifully under the tight ropes binding him to the pole in the abandoned warehouse I had brought him to after snagging his sexy ass. (I know that that sounds a bit like something out of an old fashioned cop show or movie, taking him to an abandoned warehouse, but I assure you, it was the best location I could have spirited him away to.) I snagged him right out from under everyone's noses too, fucking guy was too handsome and hunky to leave behind that was for sure. He grunted angrily now as I sucked him harder and harder, his balls crashing against my chin, me wanting to siphon yet another load from his beefy meat stick…all eight to ten inches of it buds.

"OHHHHHHHHH you fucking faggot, *you pervert!!*" he seethed and looked up at the ceiling in anguish. "Of all the fucked up things!!"

I yanked his balls down and slathered my tongue over and over them, loving the taste of his musty sweaty nuts.

"OHHHHHHHHH fucker," he grunted then, looking back down at me in astonishment, not wanting to admit to the forced ecstasy he was in, his well defined chest heaving under the binding ropes and around his torn up uniform shirt. "Easy man, easy with my damned balls you bastard!!"

His nipples were pretty sore and still erect from the way I had treated them earlier, not all that nicely let me tell you. He had two big pink fleshy nipples adorning his somewhat hairy chest, all day suckers they were. But when I got around to the main prize in his uniform pants I hadn't given it a break yet. I wondered how many women had greatly suffered his never-ending erections. The poor guy squirmed and bucked miserably in the bondage as I forced him toward yet another gusher… I was sure that he never imagined himself to be in a position like the one I presently had him in. Nor I am sure did he think he would ever be made to cum like I was forcing him to cum, vigorously siphoning load after load of security guard jazz out of him, that's just what the fuck I was doing buds. Milking a guy repeatedly and making him cum over and over seems to be some sort of well-kept secret. All you need to really do is work him every fifteen minutes to a half hour. If he is young, studly, healthy and in good shape he will be able to provide one with much enjoyment when it comes to erotically torturing his gonads…whether he is in a position to want it or not…

He was a security guard at the small drug store I had just ripped off. Actually, ripping him off as a hostage was a superb bonus let me tell you. The guy's cum tasted like sweet nectar and it seemed that he had no problem whatsoever in cooking up batch after batch of the good creamy stuff for me. All I needed to do was to keep baking his cock slowly in my mouth. I planned to suck his succulent balls dry and then to suck him some more. By the time I was done with him the handsome and hunky security guard with the black silky hair and crystal blue eyes would be in love with me…

I had needed cash in a hurry so the idea of ripping off a small establishment seemed like a really good idea. Times were bad; I was unemployed and living alone. Con jobs weren't coming my way so I succumbed to the thought of holding up a damned store. I parked my van in front of the small drug store which was on a quiet street in Brooklyn New York, left the motor running and slowly walked into the establishment. The place was not busy at all. I wondered what kind of haul I would make in a place that seemed not to draw too much business. One girl was behind the counter, one female customer was at the end of an aisle and an older looking guy, definitely the pharmacist was behind the other counter filling prescriptions. I had my handgun tucked in my belt under my jacket. I didn't see a security guard anywhere. With my heart pounding I walked up to the young girl behind the counter. She looked to be around sixteen or seventeen or so. She smiled brightly and asked if she could help me as I set a medium sized brown paper bag on the counter in front of her.

"Yeah, you can help me," I replied, trying not to sound so nervous. "I need this bag filled, with what you have in the register."

She looked at me with a puzzled expression and then I pulled my jacket back, revealing the gun in my belt.

"Oh my God," she whispered and tears filled her beautiful eyes.

"Just do as I just told you," I said softly. "Not a sound. Open the register and fill the bag. I won't hurt you."

With her hands trembling she did as I had instructed her. It was as she was filling the bag that a door at the side of the counter opened and the uniformed security guard stepped out of what was likely the bathroom. He was about six feet tall, six feet tall of utterly handsome hunk. My heart raced at the sight of him in his light blue short sleeved uniform button down shirt, black tie and tight fitting black uniform pants. Even at a glance I could tell that his muscles were straining in that shirt of his. I guessed that that was the largest size the uniform shirt came in and still he could barely fit comfortably into it, what with his bulging biceps and huge chest.

"Hey, what are you doing Lucy?" he asked the cashier when he saw her filling the bag with cash.

His voice was like velvet yet totally masculine sounding. He moved with an air of grace and fluidity as he walked. He could have been a damned model, he was that fucking beautiful, yet he chose to waste his time security guarding.

"Oh Jack!!" she cried, looking to him with tears flowing down her cheeks.

"What the fuck???" the security guard seethed and as he dashed over to her bent on rescue I pulled my gun and aimed it right at both of them.

"Okay handsome guy, not another move!" I said to him commandingly and his hands instantly went up, reaching for the ceiling. "Yeah, that's good Hero, that's really fucking good."

"Look, just take what you want and get out of here," he said, looking at me angrily.

Take what I want he said? Shit, at that moment all of a sudden HE was all I wanted. If he thought at that moment that he would soon be roped up and being milked like a steer on a farm I'm sure he would have thought he was crazy.

"Get over here handsome guy," I said to him, gesturing with the gun. "Away from the pretty girl so she can finish filling the bag for me."

He looked reluctantly at the pretty cashier, not wanting to leave her side. I wondered if they had something going on.

"I said move it Hero," I yelled at him. "You hard of hearing or something?"

As he moved from behind the counter and over to me I quickly looked around the store. The woman in the aisle was too far away from us to see what was going on and the pharmacist behind the prescription counter was staring, utterly dumbfounded.

"Okay, no one try anything and I won't hurt this handsome security guard of yours," I said meanly as the guy stood a few feet away from me, his hands still raised.

His huge chest was jutted out against his uniform shirt and his nipples were poking temptingly against it. I looked him over and saw that all he had on his belt was a pair of handcuffs.

"No gun Hero?" I asked him with a grin.

"No, no gun man," he said softly, sounding utterly defeated. "I work as an unarmed guard."

The nametag pinned on his uniform shirt read, "Jack." Looking at him in all his handsome and muscular glory I planned to do just that, to jack Jack.

"You!!" I called out to the pharmacist. "Over here, now!! Stand next to the security guard."

As the girl was almost finished filling the bag with the cash the pharmacist stepped from behind his counter and over to Jack who was shaking in his lace-up patent leather security guard shoes.

"What do you want?" the pharmacist asked me angrily but fearfully at the same time.

"Take those handcuffs off Hero's belt and lock his hands behind him," I ordered. "Hands behind you Jack."

The security guard did as I said and my cock tingled as I watched the pharmacist take the handcuffs off Jack's belt. Jack lowered his hands and placed them behind him so that the pharmacist could cuff him. I could have sworn that I saw the pharmacist glancing at and for a micro-second reaching for Jack's crotch area. I listened closely for the sounds of the cuffs locking around the hunky guy's wrists. He looked at me in total anger, a look that was bent on revenge. I could see his exquisite biceps straining at the end of his short sleeved shirt as he held his arms behind himself.

"Sorry Jack," the pharmacist said sadly.

"It, it's okay Bob," Jack said miserably. "Just do as he says."

"I'll take 'em off you after he's gone," the pharmacist said reassuringly.

"Now that won't be all that easy old man," I said, holding the gun pointed at him. "Because you see, that muscle bound security guard is coming with me when I leave here."

Jack's jaw dropped in shock and he let out a hard gulping sound as the pharmacist squeezed a hand protectively around the security guard's upper arm.

"You've got to be joking," the pharmacist said angrily, still holding tight to the guard's arm. "You can't take Jack with you."

"Ah, but I can, and I am going to old man," I said, pointing the gun now at the hunky security guard's chest. "Now, take his tie off him and blindfold him with it."

The pharmacist placed a hand woefully on the back of Jack's big neck as I turned my attention back to the girl as she finished filling the bag with cash.

"Do as he says Bob," Jack said to the pharmacist again, softly this time. "Blindfold me with my goddamned tie."

The pharmacist reached up and slowly undid Jack's tie. Watching him slide it off the guard's shirt my cock tingled more. There was something very daddy and his boy about this scene in front of me as the pharmacist was forced to restrain the security guard. As the pharmacist blindfolded the handsome security guard with the necktie I took the bag of cash from the girl behind the counter.

"Okay handsome guy, follow my voice and get the fuck over here," I said to the handcuffed and blindfolded security guard.

He slowly and cautiously made his way over to me and I grabbed him tightly by an upper arm. His fair skin felt like silk and his muscles felt like iron.

"Hmmm, strong boy you are eh?" I asked him and tucked the bag of cash into my inside jacket pocket.

"Yeah, you're real fucking lucky you got the drop on me man," he seethed angrily, looking at me with his blindfolded eyes. "I swear I would break you in two man!"

Then, holding Jack by one arm and jamming the nose of my gun into his ribs I moved slowly toward the door of the store, keeping an eye on the girl behind the counter and the pharmacist.

"Okay, you two let me and him leave here and be on our way and he just might live to see another day," I said to them threateningly. "If I see any cop cars on my tail he gets it, understand?"

The cashier and the pharmacist nodded their heads slowly. The woman in the upper aisle was totally oblivious to what was going on. At the door I hustled the security guard over to my van and quickly opened the back doors.

"Okay Hero, in you go!!" I said meanly and hauled him up into the van by the seat of his tight fitting uniform pants.

He landed slumped on the rugged floor of the van, laid out like a turkey and I slammed the doors shut, locking them. I moved fast, very fast. I pocketed my gun, got behind the driver's seat of my van and tore out of there like a bat out of hell. Because it was pretty early in the day the street was just about void of passerby at that moment. Lucky for me I suppose...

"FUCKING bastard!!" Jack ranted as he was thrown around bodily on the floor of the van as I sped through the streets.

Now the only problem I had was where was I going to take the big handsome lug? When I had decided to pull this off taking a hostage was the last thing on my mind. Where the fuck was I going to take him??? I couldn't take him back to my apartment. How the fuck would I explain a handcuffed and blindfolded security guard in the elevator? I chuckled at that thought. Half the guys in the building I live in would have loved to get their mangy hands on this fucking guy. I checked my rear-view mirror, saw that Jack was getting to his knees and abruptly spun around a side street, just to be mean to the stud. He instantly lost his balance and landed back on the van floor in a heap.

"Bastard!!" he yelled, his huge feet up in the air.

Where to go, where to go, where the fuck to go I wondered as I without thinking headed for downtown Brooklyn. When I got to the pier and water area and saw all the closed down and abandoned warehouses I stopped the van.

"Looks like as good a place as any," I said out loud, looking around the desolate area.

Again Jack pulled himself up to his knees.

"WH-where the fuck have you taken me man?" he barked at me. "If you plan on killing me do it and just get it over with huh? The thought of being a shield for the likes of you gets me sick. Fucking thief!! *Kidnapper!!*"

"Kill you Hero?" I asked him, reaching back and tousling his silky black hair. "I think not, I've brought you some place where you and I are going to have lots of fun together."

Grinning, I tugged on his shirt collar and his jaw dropped.

"Fuck man, I've been kidnapped by a damned faggot," Jack ranted. "Just what the fuck do you have in mind for me man?"

I smiled meanly, thinking of all the things I would be doing with the macho stud…

A few moments later Jack was out of the van and standing docilely as I squatted down and tied his big feet tightly together.

"Okay, looks like that place has an open door," I said, looking at the nearest of the abandoned warehouses.

I guessed that homeless people used the soon to be torn down warehouses for shelter and that was why they were open for the most part, broken open to put it more accurately. I hooked a muscular arm around and under Jack's extraordinary bubble butt and hoisted him off the ground. I leaned him halfway over my shoulder.

"FUCKER, put me down," he complained. "I'm not a sack of laundry or something."

As quickly as I could I lugged the big guy into the warehouse. I thought I was mistaken at first, but then I was sure. Jack's cock was hard and pulsing in his uniform pants, pressing against me as I carried him. I imagined it was a fear hard-on, but I would soon find out now, wouldn't I? Once inside the musty and dank smelling place I put the guy down against a large wooden pole.

"Okay, this place is perfect Hero," I said and took the necktie blindfold off him.

He looked around angrily as his eyes adjusted back to the light.

"Not a sound," I said to him threateningly.

He looked at me in total dismay and agony.

"Bet you wish you were an armed security guard huh Hero?" I asked him and unbuttoned the first few buttons of his shirt, taking in the view of his muscular and robust chest being slowly revealed to me.

"Yeah, some hero," he said miserably. "Fucking just trying to work myself through college and look what the fuck happens to me. I get my ass kidnapped by a goddamned hold-up man!"

"College boy eh?" I asked him, pulling the sides of his shirt apart, tearing them slightly and wallowing in the sight of his beautifully sculpted and muscular chest. "How old are you Hero?"

"Twenty four in a couple of day's man," he said sadly.

"Now, now, don't sound so glum about it Hero," I said and squeezed one of his nipples. "You do as you're told and I'll let you go, eventually."

I found some packaging rope and used it to get the hunky guy roped tightly to the pole that I had him leaning against. I purposely twined the rope tightly over and under his big muscular pecs, making a real nice showcase of his big fleshy pink nipples. He grimaced miserably as I tied the ropes tightly around and around his muscular torso, pinning him to the pole. In moments his upper body and legs were all tightly roped to the pole. He was fastened firmly in place, helpless to stop me from doing whatever I wanted with him...

"God man, the cops are going to find you and you're going to be locked up faster than you can spell your damned name and, OHHHHHHHHH jeez..." he gasped.

I had shut him up in mid sentence by leaning down and slurping one of his exquisite meaty nipples into my mouth. As I sucked and nipped at his left nipple I squeezed and pinched his other one with my fingertips and thumb, not being all that gentle about it either.

"OHHHHHHHH fuck, you damned faggot," he grunted loudly, his velvety voice echoing through the warehouse. "Eating and torturing my damned nips!!!"

He struggled in vain under the binding ropes, hell bent on getting free and teaching me a lesson.

"Fuck man, leave my damned nips alone huh?" he seethed as I drooled like mad over his nipple that was in my mouth.

With my fingers I twirled and tweaked his other nipple, sending chills through him as I saw goose bumps breaking out over his chest and arms.

"Fuck man, what a lousy thing to have done to me," he whimpered and heaved under the binding ropes. "First you kidnap me and now you're using me like some kind of goddamned sex toy..."

I switched my position, took his other nipple in my mouth and tweaked and teased the other one with my fingertips and thumb. Again I was not all that gentle with him. He fumed and grunted angrily.

"Damn man, I'm not a faggot," he spat at me, looking down at me working the fuck out of his great nips. "Even my damned girlfriend doesn't eat my damned nips!!"

"Then you should be thanking me Hero," I said, looked up at him and quickly slurped his nipple back into my mouth and sucked it like crazy.

The sounds of my sucking and slurping his nipples alternately filled the air around us and my gooey saliva dripped liberally down his massive chest. When I stopped working and tweaking his nipples (about twenty to thirty minutes later) they were very red and extremely erect.

"GAWD, look at what the fuck you've done to my poor nips man," he seethed, not taking notice of the fact that I was unpinning his nametag from his uniform shirt. "Fuck man, you sucked them up to the size of two bullets."

"So it would seem," I said menacingly, holding up his nametag, the pin on the back of it hanging undone.

"WH-what are you planning on doing with my nametag man?" he asked me in horror as I slowly moved it toward his left nipple. "OH FUCK, *oh fuck, on no, please man!! Don't skewer my damned nip!!*"

"I'm sure glad this area is totally deserted Hero," I said to him and pressed the tip of the needle behind his nametag against the side of his erect nipple. "Otherwise I would have had to have gagged you."

"AAAYYYYRRRR!!!!" he roared in awful pain as I slid the needle through his erect and hard nipple. "OHHHHHHH you fucking bastard!!"

With a mean looking grin on my face I clipped his nametag so that it now hung on his left erect nipple.

"OH FUCK MAN, *you fucker, you fucking pierced my damned nip with my nametag!!*" he gasped and heaved, fighting back tears of pain.

"Aren't you glad you don't have a badge Hero?" I asked him, jiggling his nametag on his nipple, sending searing pain through his body no doubt. "Just think where that might have gone..." As I spoke I teasingly glanced at his other nipple.

"AAAARRRRRRR!!! You deranged pervert, you fucking degenerate!!" he seethed as I leaned down and slurped his other nipple back into my mouth for another go round.

As I sucked his other nipple I think he was in too much pain to realize that my hand had found its way to his crotch. My own breath caught in my throat and I held his nipple meanly between my front teeth when I felt the awesome size and girth of the boner he was sporting in his tight fitting black uniform trousers.

"*Oh fuck,*" I whispered around his nipple, marveling at what I was feeling between his legs.

I stopped slurping and sucking his nipple and stood up straight in front of him, my hand over his pulsing boner. He looked beseechingly into my eyes.

"PLEASE man, take my fucking nametag off my nip," he gasped, tears now flowing down his cheeks, his exotically handsome face contorted in pain and anger, making him even more beautiful somehow.

To get his attention away from his pierced nipple I squeezed his massively sized organ through his pants.

"OOOHHHHH FUCK," he panted and slammed his head against the pole. "GAWD man, leaved my damned cock alone huh? First you went after my nips and now it's my big guy's turn huh?"

"Hero, you are in no position to be making any demands," I said to him meanly and again squeezed his throbbing hardness. "Nor are you in any position to stop me from doing whatever the fuck I want to you."

I meanly jiggled the nametag hanging on his nipple and at the same time squeezed and kneaded his manhood. Droplets of pre cum oozed through his black uniform trousers and slid down the front of them.

"Fuck man, I am going to make you cum like you won't believe," I said, leaned forward and slammed my mouth down on his hard.

His eyes opened wide in shock and revulsion as I forced my tongue far into his mouth, exploring his gums, sucking his tongue and running the tip of my tongue over his pearly white teeth. His mouth tasted of a mixture of strong coffee and mint flavored Listerine.

"RRRRRRR..." he roared as I kissed him and kissed him, squeezed his throbbing hardness through his pants and jiggled the nametag pinned to his erect nipple. "EEEeeeeeerrrrr, *y-you rastard...*"

As I kissed the fuck out of him I felt the warmth of his creamy juices staining the crotch of his pants as I squeezed the first load out of him.

"AAAAARRRRHHHH," he panted and I stopped kissing him, but went on stroking his hardness through his uniform trousers, torturing the fuck out of his pierced nipple by jiggling and jangling his nametag. "OHHHHHHHH you fucking b-bastard, g-got me creaming in my damned under shorts, fuck, FUCK, right through my uniform pants too!! OHHHHHHHHH GOD!!!"

Looking down, he seemed to be blushing in anger and mortification as I slowly but forcefully went on squeezing his manhood.

"OHHHHHHHH pervert, let go of me man!!" he seethed.

His cum was a geyser, thick, potent and creamy as it oozed and oozed through the material of his pants. When he was done the front of his pants were a mess of sticky man juices. He writhed and squealed in agony against the pole as I continued teasing his pierced nipple, tugging on the nametag, but having let go of his throbbing cock.

"OHHHHHHHH fuck, my poor nips man!!" he belted out in agony.

"Yeah, I know Hero," I said mockingly. "After you've shot that load your tits become real sensitive. Having something clipped on them makes it hundreds of times worse huh?"

Smiling meanly I jiggled the nametag some more, he looked at me through tear soaked eyes and I again slammed my mouth down on his...

"RRRRRRR..." he cried loudly as I sucked his tongue viciously into my mouth.

A few minutes later I took his nametag off his nipple. A tiny droplet of blood oozed from the hole I had made in his nub, but nothing for either of us to lose our head over. He watched in silence and with baited breath as I slowly pulled down the zipper on his uniform pants. His zipper pulled down revealed a patch of his frosty white cum sticky briefs. I smiled gleefully and he gasped as I reached past his briefs to bring out one of the biggest, fattest and juiciest cocks I had ever had the honor of seeing and touching for that matter. I brought out his balls next, not handling them all that gently I might add. They were the size of two jumbo olives in a luscious looking somewhat hairy brown sac.

"OHHHHHHHHHH fffuuuuuucccccckkk," he whispered as I held his big manhood in my hand, me looking at it in awe, twisting it a bit. "OHHHHHHH GAWD, *easy with my cock you pervert.*"

It was pulsing like a thing alive in my hand; the veins in it so fucking pronounced I could not believe it. I slowly squatted in front of the gloriously handsome stud and slurped the semi hard organ greedily into my mouth.

"OHHHHHHH fuck, *pervert!!*" he grunted down at me. "Shit man; don't be sucking me after I've just shot my damned load!! Fuck, I'm all sensitive and sexy down there right now!! OHHHHHHHHHH fuck man!!!"

He clenched his teeth as goose bumps again broke out all over him and chills coursed through his being.

"Fucking awful thing you've done man!!" he seethed as I sucked him meanly toward shooting a second load. "Shit, of all things to happen to me, I wind up kidnapped by a cock hungry faggot!"

I ran my hands up and down his long muscular legs, the muscles in them straining against the bondage he was securely tied in. He rapped his head back and forth against the pole he was tied to and grunted and panted as I sucked him and sucked him. His beautiful manhood filled my mouth and I suckled it heartily, loving the taste of his oozing pre cum. He was semi hard in my mouth and as I sucked him and sucked him he grew to a mouth-filling boner. He ranted and screamed in a man's ecstasy when I poked my tongue against his sexy piss slit and shot his load like gangbusters in my mouth.

"OHHHHHHH fuck, oh you pervert!!" he roared, drooling at the mouth as I sucked his cock as he shot another hefty load of security guard cream. "Fuck man, got me oozing a second fucking time, of all things!!"

He shook and trembled under the binding ropes as he shot rope upon rope of creamy jazz down my gullet. I gladly swallowed it all, smacking my lips and tongue around his pulsing manhood in my mouth. I tugged his sweaty balls down and he shot another good blast into my mouth.

"OHHHHHHHRRRR," he grunted throatily. "Eating my damned jazz, fucking degenerate!!"

When he was done I let his cock slip slowly from my mouth, keeping my lips securely wrapped around the tip of it for a few long seconds.

"AAAYYYYYY," he seethed as I poked his piss hole with the tip of my tongue, driving him crazier and crazier.

A few minutes later I was standing next to the trapped and tightly trussed security guard named Jack. I had tied his (necktie) blindfold back over his eyes and stood next to him holding his semi hard slimy cock in one hand as I teased and tweaked his wounded nipple, the one I had pierced earlier with his nametag.

"Bet you're wishing the cavalry would show up right about at this point eh Hero?" I asked him, twisting his nipple and stroking his cum slopped cock. "In the movies it's always about this time, when the hero can't take anymore that the cavalry shows up to rescue the poor captured guy."

"Fuck man, why don't you let me go already, huh?" he asked me, staring straight ahead with his blindfolded eyes. "Don't you think that this has gone far enough?"

In response I squeezed his nipple hard and stroked his cock faster.

"OHHHHHH GAWD, come on man, stop working my cock and wreaking havoc on my nips already!" he grunted as sweat poured down his gloriously muscular chest.

"Tell me Hero, how did a college boy wind up being a security guard in a drug store?" I asked him, still stroking and tweaking him.

"I-I need the bucks man, OHHHHHHHH, to, to pay off student loads, er-loans, OHHHHHH fuck, speak-speaking of loads h-here comes another one you bastard!!" he said breathlessly and I stroked him harder.

He shot a third load this time all over his chest and stomach regions as I held his cock pointed straight up at him. As he sluiced his load I took the blindfold off him so he could enjoy the spectacle of his energies of himself in ecstasy and at my mercy. His slop landed all over his bare chest, his stomach area and stained the sides of his pulled open uniform shirt. The fucking guy came like crazy, and for the third time at that let me tell you. It seemed that I would be able to squeeze load after fucking load out of him all fucking day, no problem whatsoever bud.

"You fucking bastard!!" he squeaked as I stepped in front of him after letting go of his shriveling cock. "N-never knew I had it in me. Never shot my damned spunk so many times in such a short period of time man, GAWD! It's like you've got magic hands and fingers!"

He spit forcefully into my face. Smiling, I ran my finger through his spittle and ate it. I repeated this four times and he looked at me in revulsion.

"Damned pervert," he whispered as I slid to my knees in front of him. "OHHHHHHH GAWD, no, no, not again you bastard!!"

He reeled and fumed as I sucked his shriveled cock, no doubt sending shockwaves through his very being...

And this is how Jack the handsome stud of a security guard wound up trapped by me in a deserted rundown warehouse. That is how he wound up being sucked of three loads and being sucked of another at this moment. By now the handsome as a prince guy was beyond sore and sweating profusely. Even though he was pretty young and robust there's just so much one cock can take...and spit forth.

"Damn it all, if I were an armed security guard this would not have happened," he squealed as I pulled meanly on his cock with my lips, tugging his balls down hard. "Fuck that, if I were a real cop this would never have even been an option!!"

His eyes opened wide in anger, terror and revulsion as he looked down at me sucking his cock and sucking his cock and sucking his cock.

"Fuck man, when are you going to let me go?" he asked desperately and tears slid down his cheeks.

It didn't take all that long for him to lay another hard-on. With my eyes closed I was in sheer heaven as I sucked the jutting piece of man-meat like crazy, running my hands up and down and up and down his long muscular legs.

"OHHHHHHHH GAWD," he murmured as I swirled my tongue around and around his manhood in my mouth. "Unbelievable man, but, I-I think I just might blast again. *I-I can't believe this shit you faggot! No woman ever got me off so many times like this!!*"

As I sucked him toward his next gusher I picked up a short length of rope from the floor. This time when he shot his load I didn't want his organ going soft. He would not believe what I had in mind next…

"OHHHHHHHHH shhhhiiiiiiiitttt!!! OH SHIT!!" he squealed loudly in a mixture of pain and ecstasy as he shot his load again into my mouth.

As I wolfed it down, sucking him like crazy at the same time I quickly wound the length of rope around the base of his balls, just under his glorious cock.

"WH-what are you doin' man?" he gasped. "T-tying up my damned cock and balls???"

When he was done shooting that fourth very painful load I stepped in front of him and grabbed his nipples, kissing him hard on the mouth. He didn't resist this time. As a matter of fact I got the feeling that he welcomed it. His lips were sweaty and salty tasting at that point, trembling a bit too as I kissed and kissed him. As planned, with his cock and balls now tightly trussed he remained hard and at attention, ready for more action. I stopped kissing him, let go of his nipples and he looked down at his pulsing erect and slimy cock before looking at me in confusion and anger.

"Damn man, wh-what are you doing to me?" he asked in awe, obviously in a state of hyper ecstasy he'd never known before. "My cock is so damned spent, yet I'm harder than concrete the way you got me here…"

Smiling, I tied his necktie back over his eyes.

"Oh man, oh no, come on man, no blindfold huh?" he pleaded.

"Okay Hero, I have to run out to the van for a minute to get something," I said and patted his chest. "Don't go away now you hear?"

Laughing, I dashed out of the warehouse and over to my van, closing the door of the place behind me.

"Fucker, don't leave me alone here like this all tied up with my damned cock on display!!" Jack shouted angrily. *"Fuck… fuck…fuck!!!"*

His hard slimy and cum coated manhood stuck out long and hard, real beefy in front of him, beads of piss and pre cum oozing from his wide sexy slit. He writhed, squirmed and strained under the binding ropes. I went back inside the warehouse a few moments later carrying a large blanket and a pair of very sharp very large cutting shears. I laid the blanket over an old but sturdy table that was at the other end of the warehouse we were in. Then I made my way over to the captured prince.

"You ready for more fun Hero?" I asked him and pulled the blindfold off him, holding up the shears for him to see.

"WH-what are you going to do with those man?" he asked, choking on his tears, obviously thinking that I was going to castrate him. "Oh my God, please man!! *Don't…"*

I put the shears under my arm and went to work undoing the ropes binding him to the pole, leaving his hands (of course) cuffed behind him.

"Pl-please man," he whimpered through clenched teeth as I took the shears from under my arm.

I squatted in front of him, his semi hard cock and balls dangling in my face and began slowly cutting his uniform pants off him, starting at the bottoms of his pants leg and working my way up. He clenched his teeth as he felt the steely side of the sheers snaking up his leg. I held tightly to his black nylon socked ankle as I slit his pants slowly off him. The cold metal of the front of the cutting shears then rubbed lovingly against his socked calf and he looked down at me in total bewilderment.

"Fuck man, what is this now?" he asked angrily. "Snippin' my damned pants off me? Shit, if you wanted to strip me why didn't you just pull them off me?"

"It's a shit-load more fun this way Hero," I said as I cut his pants at the thigh, revealing more of those sweaty, cum sticky and white briefs he was wearing.

A few minutes later the handsome prince of a security guard was stripped of his uniform pants. They lay in tatters on the floor along with his belt. Just for the fuck and fun of it I snipped his uniform shirt off him as well, leaving him wearing just his white briefs, his knee length black socks and his well-shined lace-up patent leather shoes. Stepping behind him and with my hands trembling in anticipation of what I would see where his ass was concerned I shucked his briefs down in the back, revealing two exquisite melon shaped globes of creamy back side.

"Ohhhhh man," I whispered and squeezed my palms around them, loving the silky feel of them. "God, your cheeks are hard as iron and smooth as velvet Hero."

"TH-thanks for the compliment," Jack said sarcastically.

Not able to resist I squatted behind him and pressed my lips against one of his cheeks, running my hands over his long socks and playfully snapping the elastic in them against his legs. Jeez, he had those really long OTC socks that foot fetishists all seem to love; fucking socks were kissing his knees. I parted his beautiful ass cheeks and slithered my tongue as far as possible into his gaping pink, stinking rosebud of a hole.

"OHHHHRRRR GAWD, fucking pervert," he seethed and pulled himself to his toes.

After I stopped eating and tonguing and gobbling at his hole I reached around him and grabbed his tied cock and balls. Just as I hoped for, still hard, pulsing and ready for more action. I chuckled meanly, let go of his cock and got slowly to my feet.

"G-GAWD man, n-not going to let me shoot my damned

load this time?" he spat angrily at me as I stepped in front of him.

"Starting to enjoy all this eh Hero?" I asked him and squeezed his nipples hard, twisting them.

"AAAYYYRRRRR, no way Pervert!!" he seethed, his cock oozing droplets of pre cum and twitching.

"Shit man, that cock of yours is telling another story altogether you gorgeous stud," I said, let go of his nipples and hoisted the trapped security guard up off the floor and over my shoulder.

"FUCKER, put me down and let me go already!!" he complained bitterly as I carried him over to the table that I had lain the blanket over.

A few minutes later I had the guy stretched out on the table on his back, securely tied down and he watched as I slowly stripped out of my clothes down to my thick white sweat socks. His big cock pointed straight up at the ceiling, pulsing and twitching and oozing pre cum.

"Fuck man, what do you have in mind for me now?" he asked, sounding totally irate, but looking at my muscular body in awe.

When I was standing next to him in just my white sweat socks and he was drinking in the sight of me his cock twitched like crazy. It oozed still more droplets of pre cum. It was amazing, it seemed that after the times I had jacked him off he was still able to lay a solid hard-on. I guessed that all the time I made him cum was just a warm-up to what was going to be the main event. My body is not as muscular as Jack's is but still I am in very good shape. Obviously the sight of me standing there in all my glory somehow had the guy in awe, even though he wasn't prepared to admit it.

"Liking what you see Hero?" I asked him jokingly and reached down to squeeze his nipples. "God almighty, you look like a fucking Thanksgiving turkey all stretched out and tied to that damned table."

Smiling lovingly down at him I slowly mounted the table

over his crotch, my ass cheeks spread over him.

"OHHHH fuck man, wh-what are you plannin' now???" Jack asked as my hole slid down over his big pulsing cock. "OHHHHRRRR fuck man, what kind of pervert are you anyway? Y-you're making me pork your damned hole!"

"Do it Jack, fuck my hole with your pole," I mused breathlessly as he filled my anal canal.

He seemed really reluctant at first, but his hard-on didn't deflate and then as my hole swallowed and squeezed his cock he began thrusting his hips under the binding ropes.

"OHHHHRRRR GAWD, th-this does feel great at that man," Jack seethed, looking up at me, thrusting his big manhood into me like crazy. "AAARRRHHH yeah, fucker, kidnapped me, I'll make you pay for that shit!!"

With his teeth clenched he thrust in me like a madman, making my head spin as I rode his big meat stick for all it was worth. He seemed to want to hurt me as he speared me but I think he saw that the more he attempted that the more I liked it. His balls bounced against his sweaty and sticky briefs as I rocked up and down on him, loving the feel of his huge manhood inside me.

"OHHHHHH yeah, fuck me you gorgeous stud!!" I grunted and reached down and squeezed his nipples hard.

That really seemed to set him in motion, let me tell you. He had such sensitive nips...

"FUCK, leave my damned tits alone you bastard!!" Jack panted and fucked me harder yet. "B-bastard, n-never even told me your name man!!"

I smiled down at him as he fucked me and I breathlessly said, "Ross."

"R-real nice to fucking meet you Ross," he gasped and writhed under the ropes as he went on and on fucking me. "Real nice to fuck you too man!!"

It took Jack a while longer to shoot his load that time, what with the way I had milked his cock I didn't wonder why. But I'll tell you, it was well worth the wait as he fucked me like mad. When he finally did cum he blasted a load as big as the first he had shot into my hole.

"AAAYYYRRRRR fuck, creaming in your damned hole like crazy," the security guard panted, his eyes squeezed shut as he seemed to cum and cum. "Fuck man, c-can't believe you got me cumming like this!!"

As he shot his load I grabbed my hard cock and stroked it, shooting my own load over his gloriously muscular chest and splattering his nipples with it.

"OHHHHHH yeah, fucking gorgeous guy you are Jack," I panted.

When we were both done I slowly slid off his cock, shuddering as I went and climbed down off the table. Jack's cock remained hard and erect due to the rope still tied around it. He looked up at me with desperation showing in his eyes as I leaned down to slurp my cum off his big fleshy nipples.

"Ross," he whispered.

"I know Jack, oh God, what the fuck are we going to do?" I whispered as we looked at each other helplessly, he because he was still tied tight and me because looking at him filled me with a feeling of love I had never known before.

I began untying the ropes holding the guy to the table, but left his hands cuffed behind him...

About fifteen minutes later I was dressed and I had the guy standing against the pole he had been tied to earlier. His hands were still cuffed behind him, I had tied his feet securely together and he was blindfolded. I held him close to me, kissing his cheek, his earlobe and neck.

"I'll call the drugstore and tell them where you are," I said to him, kissing him and packing his cock and balls into his briefs. "They'll send the cops to get you out of here."

"Ross please," Jack whispered and I kissed his cheek.

"No Jack, no," I whispered and kissed him again, tugging on the knot in his blindfold.

I was glad I had blindfolded the guy. I didn't want him seeing my tears. Before walking out of the warehouse I squeezed a small scrap of paper into his hand.

"Don't let anyone see that when they come to get you," I said softly and dashed out of the warehouse and to a pay-phone.

I dialed information, got the phone number for the drug-store and told the girl that I had ripped off where Jack could be found. I got into my van and high-tailed it out of there like a bat out of hell.

When the police arrived to free Jack he kept his fist tightly closed. They wrapped the guy in a blanket and drove him to his apartment, after they were convinced that no damage had been done to him...

Two nights later I was sitting in my apartment watching TV, dressed in just my underpants and sweat socks when I heard a knock at the door. Grinning from ear to ear I stood up and not bothering to put on pants I padded to the door. Without looking through the peephole to see whom it was I opened the door. He stood there looking glorious and handsome in tight fitting jeans, black work boots and a button down white shirt.

"You owe me a uniform Fucker," he said meanly.

Without hesitation I grabbed him by the sides of his shirt, hauled him into the apartment, kicked the door shut and slammed him against a wall, my lips quickly finding his. As I kissed him I reached into his pocket and brought out his handcuffs.

"Looking for a repeat performance huh Hero?" I asked him, spinning him around and locking his hands behind him. "Fuck man, I'm going to milk you all night long you stud!!"

He grinned from ear to ear as I tied a blindfold on him.

"Shit man, you can milk me all you want, just as long as I get to fuck that bung-hole of yours a few times," Jack said as I hauled him to my shoulder and carried him to my bedroom.

I didn't let the guy go till two days later...

A Boner Book

The Hustler

"Why do hustlers wear so much white?" he asked me as I sat against his body, wearing just my short white boxer briefs.

My big, thick cock and hairy plum sized balls were sticking out of the fly opening in my briefs. His naked body was wrapped around mine and as he leaned against my back he reached around me and squeezed, twisted, pinched, teased the fuck out of, and pulled on my big pink fleshy jutted up nipples.

"Tell me, why do hustlers wear so much white?" he asked me again, sounding breathless as his hard and erect cock pressed against my lower back, his lips right against my ear as he spoke, his tongue teasing my inner ear. "When I met you at the bar you were wearing white jeans and now I see you had on white underpants as well. So, tell me, why do you wear so much white?"

I smiled before replying, a smile that had won me more than a good share of rich and very well to do clients.

"That was the same goddamned question Tony Ward was asked in that movie Hustler White," I said as I stroked my hard pulsing organ, his lips now pressed against the back of my big neck. "Purity I suppose is one reason. Personally, I just think it looks kind of sexy."

He gave my nipples a hard tug at that point, causing me to clench my teeth in pain and to grab my cock even tighter as I stroked myself toward a third jazz shot. That tug he gave my nipples knocked my killer smile off my face real fucking quick let me tell you. My first two shots of creamy cum had already dried up and were caked up on my muscular hairy chest. I would need a good hot shower when this was over, that was a definite.

"What is your name?" he whispered in my ear and gave

my earlobe a fast nip with his front-most teeth.

"Told you man, my name is Steve," I replied breathlessly as I stroked myself faster, grunting and sweating as I did so, the muscles in my biceps and triceps bulging.

"So you said," he whispered and ran the tips of his fingers over my nipples and grabbed them again. "A beautiful name for a beautifully handsome man, you were well named Steve."

His fingers were driving my nipples beyond crazy at that moment. He had been at it for over an hour at that point. Never before had a client wanted so much to play with and erotically torture my damned tits. But he was a client after all, the money was good, and I wasn't one to argue with what the customer wanted. I mean, okay, there were certain things even as a hustler that I would not do, but this was reasonable in its own way. I stroked my cock faster still and he gave my nipples another of those hard painful tugs. I gasped in pain just as he would have wanted me to.

"What made you choose this line of work?" he asked me, running the palms of his hands over and under my pecs before quickly resuming his torture of my nipples. "What makes such a beautiful young man want to be a hustler?"

"Good money," I panted as I felt myself getting close to cumming a third fucking time. "And I like to meet interesting people. OHHHHHHRRRR GOD, yeah…"

His hard cock rubbed and rubbed against my lower back and he held onto me tighter and tighter, hugging the fuck out of me, loving me in a sadistic manner, and really, *really* driving my nipples batty with what he was doing to them. By now my nubs were swollen and tingling on my muscular and well-toned hairy chest.

"How old are you Steve?" he asked me softly, pulling hard on the very tips of my nipples, twisting them hard.

"AAAARRRRRRR, I-I'm twenty-three," I grunted breathlessly and in erotic pain.

I grabbed my cock tighter and tighter, causing myself pain also. We had been at it for better than an hour at that point. More than an hour since the man who had not yet told me his name picked me up in the hustler bar called "The Big H Spot." I had been wearing a pair of tight white jeans, a black string style tank top, and black Western boots. I was sitting at the end of the bar sipping an ice cold beer when he walked into the place.

"Getting close to number three?" he asked me, sounding sort of mocking.

"Yes, yes I am," I replied, sweating profusely now and straining as I stroked my cock fast, shaking in his loving grasp as he squeezed my poor nipples hard.

My nipples had never felt so sore before in my life.

"When you're done you'll take a Viagra and then go for a fourth," he whispered and kissed the back of my neck, running his tongue over the short hairs back there.

"OH GOD," I gasped. "A-another one? Again man???"

It was what he was paying me for after all. At the bar the bartender had placed a fresh beer in front of me and told me it was from the gentleman at the end of the bar. I glanced up and looked at him before taking the mug of beer in my hand. Taking the drink in my hand would tell him that I had accepted his proposal. Not taking the drink in my hand would tell him I was not interested. That was the unspoken way of lining up clients at "The Big H Spot." He was drop-dead handsome, wearing a navy blue business suit. His hair was dark brown; cut in what I would call a banker's cut and he had beautiful dark eyes. He looked to be as tall as I am, about six feet. I took the beer in hand, raised it, smiled across at him, and took a long chugging sip of it. As I sipped the beer I wondered what a handsome dude like him would want with a hustler. I guessed maybe he was one of those married Wall Street bulls and just wasn't in the mood for the wife that particular night. More than likely he had called her to tell her he would be stuck late at the office, the office being "The Big H Spot" at the moment.

"OHHHRRRRR GOD, yeah, I'm cumming now," I gasped as he held me tighter, squeezing my nipples harder yet. "AAAAAAARRRR SHIT…SHIT…got me jazzing like a madman here Mister…"

My cum spurted from my cock slit in long thick creamy ropes, landing on my chest, and dripping down toward my washboard-like stomach. When I was done spewing my load he didn't let go of my nipples. Instead he hurt them more and more. If you are a guy like me your body tends to become super sensitive after shooting a hefty load. After having shot a load the last thing I want is for anyone to be squeezing my nipples, seeing as they become the most sensitive feeling part of me after I've let off a nice load of ball juice, but this fucking guy was the customer after all, and it was what he was paying for.

"OOOHHHRRRR my poor nips," I roared breathlessly.

"Go for it again you gorgeous bastard," he said just above a whisper and his cock rubbed against my lower back, oozing pre cum on me.

I hadn't even let go of my cock and I was again stroking it, sending chills through my muscular body, goose bumps breaking out all over me. He chuckled fiendishly and placed two fingers to my lips, slipping a tiny Viagra pill into my mouth. I chewed it vigorously, stroked my cock and sweated like crazy.

When I had placed my beer on the bar he was standing next to me. The scent of his cologne was overwhelming, real sexy, and up close I could see that he was extremely handsome. His big dark eyes seemed to be piercing me. I guessed his age to be around thirty-three or so.

"Hi, thanks for the beer," I said and smiled at him.

"You're very welcome," he replied, his beautiful eyes seeming to drink me in as they looked over my chest.

"I'm Steve," I said, holding out my hand for him to shake.

He took my hand in his, held it tight, and with his other hand he pulled the front of my tank top away from my chest.

"You don't mind do you Steve?" he asked me as he looked down at my revealed pink, meaty and pointy nipples.

"No, I guess not man," I said sheepishly. "You could uh, maybe tell me your name though. I mean, I would like to properly thank you for the beer."

He let go of my tank top, it snapped back against my chest and he said, "You will, and my name is not important, or at least not at the moment." He let go of my hand and glanced at the vacant bar stool next to me.

"Have a seat," I said and took a sip of my beer.

As I stroked myself hard again he relentlessly squeezed, pinched, twisted and pulled at my poor nipples. The Viagra had taken its effect and I was hard and pulsing again.

"OHHHHRRRR," I groaned. "Fucking A man, number four is being cooked up now in my big sweaty nuts!"

He sat down next to me, crossed his leg over his knee and picked up my beer bottle. He held it to my lips and right there at the bar, in front of everyone I allowed him to feed me the beer. I sipped it down and placed the tips of my fingers on his (black) socked ankle, the feel of his nylon sock against his hard leg sending chills up my spine. When it comes to fetishes I'll admit I'm a sucker for a handsome guy in black socks and shined shoes.

"I want to discuss something with you Steve," he said to me, moving the half-empty bottle away from my lips. "An offer, so to speak."

I looked at him with eyes filled with lust and he smiled mockingly at me.

"What is it you want to discuss?" I asked him, my fingers moving under his pants leg.

He put the mouth of my beer bottle under his nostrils and sniffed it, taking in the scent of my lips that I had left on it. A look of ecstasy came over his face. He breathed deeply, put the bottle down on the bar, and again pulled the top of my tank-top away from my chest, further this time, revealing my nipples for anyone who wanted to see them.

"My, but don't they look delicious," he said breathlessly, looking at the two pink cheery-like nubs on my chest. "I could devour nipples like that, really put them to the test."

"Are you talking about my tits?" I asked him, glancing down at my nubs as he seemed to be reveling in the sight of them. "I love to have them slurped at man."

With a mean looking grin on his face he let go of my tank top, it again snapped back against my chest and he calmly took my hand off his socked ankle.

"Hey man," I said, sounding offended.

"So Steve, how much to have you come back to my apartment and let me work and play with those delectable nipples of yours till my heart is content?" he asked me.

"That depends man," I said and took my bottle of beer in hand. "What exactly is it that you want to do with my tits?"

"Work them, play with them, and hold you as you pleasure yourself repeatedly," he replied as I took a sip of my beer. "You are magnificent looking to the point that I would most likely want to hold onto you for more than a few hours. I will feed you Viagra tablets when needed...so you can pleasure yourself over and over for me."

As he tortured my nipples it was going on our second hour together. I stroked myself like crazy, willing myself to make myself cum a fourth time for him, sweating like crazy by now, really dripping with it. The Viagra he had given me had really helped me to rise to the occasion real soon again.

"You mean to say you want to watch me jack myself off as you work my tits man?" I asked him and put my bottle of beer on the bar in front of me.

"Yes," he replied, took my hand in his two, and moved it back to where I had had it on his socked ankle a few moments ago.

The tips of my fingers trailed along his nylon black dress sock and my breath came in pants.

"How much Steve?" he whispered, and was looking hungrily at my chest.

"I charge four hundred dollars an hour," I replied.

"For each hour you stay with me while I work your nipples you will receive five hundred dollars Steve," he said and picked up my beer bottle.

He again sniffed the mouth of my beer bottle, taking in the scent of my lips as my hand moved up and under his pants leg.

I found the top of his calf length sock and playfully snapped the elastic of it against his leg.

"But, you must continue to pleasure yourself all through-out the ordeal as I work and play with your wonderful looking nipples Steve," the man said very softly and put the mouth of my beer bottle to my lips.

I puckered my lips around the mouth of the bottle, stuck out my tongue, and dribbled saliva onto the bottle, giving him some of me to really sniff at.

"Even if we get to more than three or four hours you will not let go of your member, and I will not let go of your nipples, except of course to feed you a Viagra tablet if needed," he said and tipped the bottle so I could get a sip of my beer. "Do we have an agreement Steve?"

I nodded "yes" and he pulled the bottle from my lips. I watched as he sniffed the mouth of the bottle as my fingers found their way under his black dress sock that I was still toying with.

"If you pleasure yourself enough times and you endure me working your nipples relentlessly I will give you those socks I'm wearing as a bonus," he said and gulped down what was left of my beer. "Something to always remember me by so to speak."

I smiled. He put the now empty beer bottle down on the bar, I took my hand off his socked ankle and we smiled at each other. I held out my hand, signaling him that we were in business. He shook my hand, holding onto it with a strong and firm grip.

"Shall we be on our way?" he asked me. "I have a car waiting for us outside."

"Sure thing," I said and stood up.

He took me by my upper arm and held it tight as we walked to the exit of the bar.

"See you tomorrow Ted," I said to the bartender as I walked with the nameless man.

Ted, the bartender who looks out for all the hustlers that work his bar smiled at me, waved, and got a real good look at my client. (Just in case...) Outside the bar it was a warm and balmy July afternoon. Outside, the man quickly released his hold on my arm. A small part of me was wondering if I was doing the right thing here. He still hadn't told me his name after all. The man's car was actually one of those corporate cabs, a mini limousine so to speak. The mini limousine had dark tinted windows, so no one outside the car could see who was inside the car. A driver dressed in a dark colored suit and a chauffeur's cap stepped out of the car. He was about five feet nine inches tall. He had dark eyes, a thick mustache, and from what I could see of his hair under his cap it was dark and curly.

"Good evening Sir," the chauffeur said to the nameless man. "Are we ready to be on our way?"

"Yes we are Charles, we are ready," the man said to the chauffeur. "Charles, this is Steve. He will be accompanying me home tonight."

"A pleasure to meet you Steve," the chauffeur said politely, shook my hand, and opened the back door of the car.

My nameless client gestured for me to get into the car first. I climbed in and saw a mini bar in front of the back seat, along with a television and a phone. The nameless man climbed into the car, sat down next to me, and Charles closed the door of the car. Charles got into the driver's seat of the car but did not immediately begin driving. The nameless man produced a long white silk scarf from his suit jacket pocket. He folded it in half and held it up to my face.

"I am going to blindfold you for the ride Steve," he said to me. "Don't be frightened. Its just a precaution."

I sat docilely still as he tied the silk blindfold over my eyes.

"It's really best that you don't know where I live Steve," he said.

"S-sure," I replied nervously.

As I thought of him tying that silk blindfold on me my cock became rage hard. I knew I would have no problem shooting that fourth load for him real soon...and of course the Viagra he'd fed me helped me along as well. I stroked my cock more and more.

"All right Charles, we're ready now," the man said to the

chauffeur and the car started.

"Who are you man?" I whispered breathlessly. "Who are you that I have to be blindfolded for the ride to your place?"

"As I said in the bar Steve, my name is not important," the man said and leaned in close to me. "Now, I would like a sample of what I am paying for. Remove your tank top please."

I did as he told me and when I was shirtless I felt his fingers gently moving over my big nipples. They became erect and hard at his touch.

"Exquisite," he whispered in a very feminine sounding tone of voice.

As we drove on I felt the tips of his fingers toying with the knot in my blindfold and trailing over it where my eyes were. A couple of times he stuck a finger or two in my mouth and I dutifully sucked them. His fingers and hands always found their way back to my nipples though. They were his obsession.

About a half-hour or so later the car came to a slow halt and I heard the sound of a garage door being opened via remote control. All through the ride the nameless man had gently run his fingertips over my nipples, my pecs, and my hugely muscular chest. He had not yet started squeezing, pinching, twisting and really torturing the guys yet. My cock was rock hard in my white jeans. The car moved into the garage and then I heard the garage door sliding shut.

"Okay Sir, it's safe now," I heard Charles say.

My nameless client took the blindfold off me and placed it back in his suit jacket pocket. I rubbed my eyes and let them adjust to the dimly lit garage.

"I do apologize for having to have made you wear the blindfold Steve," he said to me, giving one of my nipples a gentle rub.

"No problem man, you're the boss after all," I said.

Charles opened the door of the car and we stepped out. I had my tank top in my hand as the nameless man took me by my upper arm. We were in a garage and from what I could tell there was a door that connected the garage to the house. We were definitely no longer in Manhattan that was for sure.

"Charles, be here at eleven thirty PM sharp," the man said to the chauffeur. "I think by that time Steve here will be ready to return to "The Big H Spot.""

"Yes Sir," the chauffeur replied with respect. "Steve, it was a pleasure meeting you."

The chauffeur held out his hand, I shook it as he stole a lustful glance at my bared chest, and then allowed my client to walk me through the door as he held my arm tight.

The house was beautiful to say the least. I looked around at the luxurious surroundings as he walked me into a huge living room. Against one wall was a tremendous entertainment center, complete with a wide screen television, a VCR, a DVD player and an elaborate stereo system. Against another wall was a complete wet bar. The walls were painted beige and were adorned with large pictures directly from a gallery I was sure.

"You are impressed I take it?" he asked me and let go of my arm.

"Yes Sir, I am," I replied as he walked over to the bar.

"Beer?" he asked me.

"Uh, yes, thank you," I replied as I stood there with my tank top in my hand, wondering just who the hell my client was that he was able to afford all this plus a chauffeur driven car.

"You may remove your boots, jeans and socks now," he said to me as he stood behind the bar, looking at me across the room. "But please be sure to leave your under shorts on. You are wearing under shorts are you not Steve?"

"Yeah, sure," I said, dropping my tank top on the floor and reaching down to get one of my black boots off..

As I did as I was told he took a bottle of beer from the refrigerator under the bar. He took the cap off it and watched as I slowly pushed my white jeans down to my ankles, revealing the short white boxer briefs I was wearing and my calf length white sweat socks. I stepped out of my jeans, reached down again, this time to pull my socks off and stood there in my under shorts facing him. My cock was rage hard in my under shorts and pressing against them, demanding release. Droplets of pre cum seeped through the material of my under shorts.

"Magnificent," he muttered and walked over to me, the beer bottle clutched in his hand. "Truly, truly magnificent..."

When we were standing inches apart he put the mouth of the bottle to my lips and allowed me to have a fast chugging sip. I stood there as he ran the mouth of the bottle over my lips, holding tight to my arm as he did so. I licked and kissed the bottle as if it were a cock.

"Truly magnificent," he said again and ran the top of the bottle over my nipples.

"Like those tits of mine eh?" I asked him.

"How many times do you think you can make yourself cum repeatedly Steve?" he asked me, not answering my question.

"Well, that depends on what's being done to make me cum," I replied and he smiled tauntingly at me. "And of course after I've cum a few times I might need a little pick-me-up, ala Viagra..."

"Good answer Steve," he said and gave one of my nipples a hard squeeze, sending a fast chill through me. "Now, take that meat and your balls out of the fly opening in your under shorts, place your hands behind you and kneel down on the floor."

Again I did as I was told. I reached into my short boxer briefs, pulled my hard cock and plum sized hairy balls out of the fly opening and let go of them. My cock pointed straight up, long, hard, and pulsing. My big balls hung down real low and juicy looking. Looking at my nameless client, as he stood there with the beer in his hand, his eyes practically boring into me, I crossed my wrists behind my back and kneeled down in front of him. My eyes were looking right at his crotch. When he took a step toward me I stole a kiss on his crotch. Smiling down at me he held the top of the beer bottle to my lips. I wrapped my lips around the mouth of the bottle and he fed me the beer, tilting the bottle. I sipped it down. Then, he grabbed me by the back of my neck, tilted the bottle higher and forced me to guzzle the beer.

"RRRMMMFFFF..." I said as the beer flooded my mouth

and throat, trying desperately to swallow every drop.

"Don't spill a drop you gorgeous hunk,"he said in a threatening tone of voice.

He didn't let me stop to catch my breath. Instead he force-fed me the entire bottle of beer. When the beer was gone he made me suck on the neck of the bottle, thrusting it in and out of my mouth like it was a cock. When he finally took the bottle out of my mouth I sat there on my knees catching my breath. I looked up at him as he trailed his fingers under my chin, toying with my black neatly trimmed goatee, pulling on it a little.

"Are you all right?" he asked me, but not with sympathy in his voice.

"Yes Sir," I gasped and licked my beer tasting lips.

"You know who is in charge Steve," he said and ran a hand through my thick black hair.

"Yes Sir, you are in charge," I said respectfully.

"Another beer?" he asked me, grinning down at me and tugging on my mustache.

"If you say so Sir," I responded with the utmost respect.

He walked to the bar, got another bottle of beer and forced me to guzzle that one down also, not letting me breathe as I gulped and guzzled it. When I was done I had consumed four large beers at that point, the first two at the bar and two more while I was on my knees in front of him. My cock pulsed like crazy and the need to piss was setting in good and heavy.

"My bedroom is upstairs Steve," he said to me, stepping away from me and placing the empty beer bottles on top of the bar. "Shall we?" He gestured toward a flight of stairs and I stood up. Holding my upper arm in a firm grasp he walked me up the long flight of stairs to his spacious bedroom. I was slightly lightheaded, but definitely not drunk from the four beers I had consumed. His bed was a king-size job. As I looked around the bedroom he held tightly, almost lovingly to my arm and my cock pulsed like crazy, beads upon beads of cum and piss forming at the tip of it.

"Who are you?" I whispered, looking in awe around the

beautiful bedroom.

He smiled, pulled me close to himself and kissed me gently on the lips, grabbing my succulent butt cheeks through my boxer briefs.

"May I uh, use the bathroom?" I asked him. "I really have to uh, piss."

"After you've undressed me," he said, letting go of me and taking two small steps away from me.

I nodded and helped him out of his suit jacket, taking on the role of a humble servant it seemed. The tag on the inside of the jacket read Armani. He pointed to a chair and I hung the jacket neatly over the back of it. Next, I slowly undid his necktie, slid it off his shirt and held it in my hand as I unbuttoned his crisp white shirt. My cock throbbed like a thing alive as I slowly undressed him. I helped him out of his shirt, revealing a muscular, hairless chest with two small pink nipples adorning it. I looked at them hungrily.

"All this talk of tits has made me crazy for them Sir," I said with a grin.

He nodded "no" and pointed to the chair. I placed his shirt and tie on the back of the chair with his suit jacket as he walked over to the bed and sat down on the end of it. I went over to him and knelt in front of him on one knee, a position he seemed to really thrive on having me in. I leaned over and slowly unlaced his right wingtip, my mouth filling with saliva. Before slipping his right shoe off his foot I leaned down further and kissed the tip of it, running my tongue gingerly over it. He gently caressed the back of my neck as I slipped his shoe off him. The sight of his black socked foot drove me wild. My cock pulsed harder yet, aching to cum. I lifted his socked foot to my face and licked the sides of it, the meaty bottom of it, and sucked the sweaty juices from his socked toes for a few seconds. The smell and taste of his sock was funky and overpowering all at the same time. He was watching me intently as I slobbered over the top of his socked foot and quickly slurped it up. I looked up at him as he gestured with his eyes at his other foot. I quickly reached under his pants leg, yanked his right sock off his foot and began unlacing his left wingtip. Snickering he told me to take care of his left foot with my tongue. I didn't need special instructions. I leaned down and using my teeth unlaced his wingtip. I kissed it a few times before taking it off his foot. Getting his sock off with my teeth required a tad more work but I did it, beginning at pulling the front-most part of his sock away from his toes with my teeth first. As I did that I was able to again suck the musty foot smell from his sock.

A few moments later he was standing over me bare footed as I knelt there undoing the belt buckle on his suit trousers. I unbuttoned his suit trousers and they fell down, pooling around his ankles, revealing a pair of frosty white briefs, a huge piece of tube steak in them, it pulsing like mine and oozing pre cum. I also saw what looked like small piss stains on the front of his briefs. As he stepped out of his suit trousers I pressed my nose and mouth against his briefs and inhaled deeply. I smelled an erotic mixture of piss, pre cum, and man sweat. I flicked my tongue out of my mouth and lapped at his pre cum and piss stains on his briefs. He hadn't told me not to so I went ahead and indulged myself. The guy crooned and moaned contentedly, reaching down to caress the back of my neck.

"I want those nipples Steve," he whispered breathlessly. "Finish the task at hand and then we'll get started."

"Y-yes Sir," I replied and grabbed the sides of his briefs.

He was totally naked then, his big cock pointing straight out at me, long, hard, beefy and pulsing. I slowly got to my feet and stood before him in my white boxer briefs. The need to piss was now beyond overwhelming.

"Where is the bathroom Sir?" I asked him politely.

Smiling wickedly he squatted in front of me and took just the very tip of my hard manhood in his mouth. He nodded that it was okay.

"OHHHHHHHRRRRR GOD," I grunted breathlessly and pissed in his mouth, my urine coming out in spurts. "Can't believe this man, first client ever to gulp down my frothy piss."

He gulped my warm rancid piss down his gullet the way I

had guzzled the beer. He sucked the tip of my cock and it drove me crazy to tell the truth. Goose bumps sprang up all over my body as I pissed and pissed in his mouth with him sucking the crown of my big cock. Pissing with the tip of your cock wedged in someone's mouth can really make a guy piss long and slow. As I stood there with the tip of my tube steak in his mouth I again pissed in long spurts. It felt like I would never stop pissing.

"Mmmmmmm..." he crooned as he drank my piss.

He sucked the tip of my cock like crazy, making me shudder and do a stupid looking dance as I stood there. When I was done he stood up facing me. My cock remained super hard and he reached out and grabbed my nipples hard. I placed my wrists behind me as he began twisting, squeezing, pinching and pulling hard on my nipples, really hurting them a few times.

"AAAYYYRRRR..." I grunted as he began pulling me toward the bed by my nipples.

"Grab your cock and start stroking it you hunk of meat," he said in a nasty tone of voice. "Remember, the longer you stay here and the more you cum the more money you'll make."

"I-I'll remember Sir," I croaked, walking on my tiptoes as he forced me along by my nipples.

So, we sat on the bed with me in front of him and him wrapped around my body, reaching around me and toying relentlessly with my nipples as I stroked myself to orgasm after orgasm. Each time I shot my load it landed all over my chest and my nipples suffered more after each time I came.

"OHHHHHH yeah man," I said as I sat there drenched in sweat now, my nipples sore to his touch and my cock feeling numb and tingling as I stroked the guy toward gusher number four.

"Getting close to number four eh Steve?" he asked me and nipped at one of my earlobes. "That Viagra pill I gave you sure helps. I love to torture a man's nipples as he strokes and pleasures himself."

"Glad to hear it man, but my tits sure are feeling really blasted now," I gasped. "I-I think number four should do it for me

Sir. OHHHHHHH, oh my God, yeah…getting there Sir!"

"I'm sure you can coax a fifth shot from yourself Steve," he whispered in my ear. "You must push yourself past these limits you've created for yourself. I do have more Viagra as well."

As he spoke he really squeezed my nipples hard and I spewed a fourth, but small mess of cum from my cock slit.

"AAARRRRRHHH yeah, fucking yeah…" I gasped loudly, leaning against him, my head back on his shoulder.

His cock rubbed against my lower back, still hard, still pulsing like crazy. I felt a mess of pre cum on my back as he went on, *still* working my now swollen jutted up nipples.

"OHHHHHRRRR," I grunted wildly when I was done shooting my fourth load. "Pl-please man, let go of my tits already! You-you're making me crazy!"

My hair was sweat soaked and hanging over my forehead. I was shaking like a leaf and I didn't dare push his hands away. Frenzied as he had me he was still a client. I gasped, bucked and heaved for breath and stroked my poor cock. He kissed the back of my neck a few times, his mustache tickling me a bit back there.

"When you shoot load number five I will shoot my load as well," he whispered, sounding lustful as all hell. "All over your glorious and muscular back, but not until you've climaxed a fifth time Steve."

"OHHHHHHHHRRRR *shit…*" I croaked in a high pitched tone of voice.

My poor cock was beyond numb at that point and it was tingling like mad, wondering what the fuck was going on, wanting for me to let go of it already. My nameless client palmed his hands over my nipples and squeezed hard.

"AAAYYYYYRRRR SHIT!!" I roared in anger and ecstasy all at once. "Pain and pleasure huh you fucker? What a twisted combo I gotta say…"

"Come on Steve, a fifth one for me," he whispered demandingly and as I squeezed my eyes shut I felt a tiny pill slipped into my mouth.

With my lips trembling I chewed the Viagra and gulped it down.

"AAARRRHHHHHHH..." I gurgled loudly as he gripped the tips of my nipples with his thumbs and first two fingers, kneading and spinning them.

He wrapped his legs around me, his smelly bare feet directly under my crotch. I stroked myself harder and as the Viagra kicked in a short while later my hand and cock made squishing sounds. But it was as I looked at his feet that did it; my cock grew rigidly stiff in my hand as I stroked it faster and faster. I glanced over at his black dress socks on the floor where I had left them after having pulled them off him. I looked at his bare feet under my crotch. I grew harder and harder in hand.

"T-tell me again Sir," I panted wildly.

"Tell you what Steve?" he asked, his lips pressed lightly against my back as he teased and tormented the fuck out of my nipples.

"Tell me again how besides the money you'll pay me I'll be able to keep the socks you were wearing as a souvenir of all this," I said breathlessly.

He chuckled lightly, gave my nipples a hard slap each, and said, "Of course Steve, you may have my socks. You will certainly have earned them." At the sound of those words I erupted a fifth time, shooting my load.

"OHHHHHHHHHHH!!!" I gasped and bucked against his body as he held me tighter and tighter, squeezing the beef of my nipples.

"Yes Steve, that's it, *that's it,*" he panted and then I felt his load shooting against my back as he rocked against me. "Ohhhhhhh yes...yessssssss Steve..."

He hissed like a snake and nipped at the back of my neck, as he seemed to cum and cum and cum like crazy. I wondered how many days of spunk he had stored up in his balls. His cum landing on my back felt hot, thick and creamy. When I was done shooting my fifth load I sat there still as a statue, holding my soft cock in my hand as he breathed heavily behind me, his hands resting gently on my pecs.

"How do you feel Steve?" he whispered.

"Wiped Sir," I replied. "I feel totally wiped out, yet I feel great at the same time."

I was literally sopping wet in sweat, tingling all over, my nipples were the size of two over-sized cherries and my cock was numb beyond reason. I smelled of a mixture of sweat and cum and my entire body was feeling super sensitized.

"If it's okay with you Sir I'll take my money now and those socks of yours and be on my way," I began to say when he grabbed my nipples with his thumbs and first two fingers, *again.*

"AYYYRRRRRR OH my GOD," I gasped as he gave them a hard yank followed by a twist. *"Please Sir..."*

I looked down, and at the sight of the guy's hands torturing my nipples all over again he had me stroking myself like a mad-man. It was as if he now had me programmed. If he squeezed my nipples I instantly stroked my manhood. He held me super tight and I felt his juices spewing on my back as he shot a second load.

"Stoke that cock of yours Steve," he whispered harshly in my ear, the tip of his tongue burrowing into my ear. "I want to watch you suffer..."

"Who the fuck are you man???" I seethed as I did as he said.

This time I didn't cum. I simply roared like a trapped animal as my aching balls bounced up and down on the bed as he went on and on torturing my nipples. I sat there shaking like a leaf when he *still* didn't let go of my nipples.

"AAAAAARRRRR SHIT," I thundered as I suffered a dry load. "N-never met someone so hot for my tits Sir."

My body was a mess of goose bumps; I was sensitive all over to the least little touch and realized that I had been hired by a sadistic and torturous man. He held my nipples tight, squeezed the bejesus out of them, twisted them and commanded me to stroke myself. I croaked in a high pitched tone of voice and did as I was told... I bucked and heaved in his grasp on my tits on the bed. I pressed my feet against the bed and arched my muscular and sweaty body as he fondled the fucking fuck out of my poor overused nipples.

"AAAAARRRRRR..." I gasped miserably, feeling insane with it all by then. "S-suffering for you now Sir..."

Later, more than two hours later to be totally honest I was lying on the man's bed on my back, looking up at the ceiling. My nipples were two swollen and over-ripe cherries on my chest, my cock hung flaccid and exhausted out of the fly opening in my boxer briefs, and my body was a mess of gelled cum and sweat all over me. As I lay there completely exhausted my nameless client was standing by his large dresser, pulling on a pair of long silk pajama-like pants.

"I want to thank you for a wonderful evening Steve," he said and walked over to the bed, looking down at me. "My driver will take you back to the bar now, or wherever you wish to go. I doubt you are in any shape to be servicing anymore clients tonight."

Smiling wickedly he leaned down and gave each of my nipples a hard twist.

"Ohhhhhh..." I moaned softly.

A little while later I was dressed and standing in the garage with Charles the driver. My tank top was irritating my nipples but I didn't want to not wear it. I didn't want anyone to see the shape my nipples were in.

"The man treated you well then?" Charles asked me as he tied the silk blindfold over my eyes.

"Yeah, you could say that," I replied as he guided me into the car.

As Charles drove I realized that I had not found out my client's name.

Back at the bar I walked up to the bartender with more than two thousand dollars (in cash I might add) in my pocket. Ted saw me and came over to where I was standing. I reached into a pocket of my white jeans and brought out the black socks that my client had also given me. I slammed them down on the bar and Ted smiled at me.

"Another pair of client's socks you horny fuck?" Ted asked me.

"Sure thing man," I replied and tucked the prized socks back into my pocket. "And per our bet you owe me a beer on the house."

Ted placed a cold beer in front of me and I gulped it down greedily. Shit I was thirsty...

Milked

A Boner Book

About the Author

Christopher Trevor was born in July 1963 and grew up in New York City. As soon as he was old enough to know how he began writing fiction and has been writing gay erotic/fetish stories for the past ten to twelve years at this point. He became an avid reader as well from the time he knew how and reads everything from fiction, to non-fiction to biographies of interesting and unusual people, people who have made a difference or who have paved the way for others. Christopher attributes his writing artistic inspiration to artists such as  Etienne, Tom of Finland, Tagame, The Hun, and most notably Joe T, who Christopher has had the pleasure of speaking with and even meeting over the last few years. Christopher states, "Joe T encouraged me to write about my fetish because I was embarrassed about it at the time. Joe T said that when we are embarrassed about something that makes it even more enticing somehow." Christopher totally agreed and never stopped writing in this genre. Erotic writers who inspired Christopher Trevor were: Tom Shaw (author of "That Day at the Quarry), C.S. White (author of Big Sur), Larry Townsend (author of countless erotic novels), and Mason Powell (author of the classic story "The Brig.")

Christopher discovered that not only did he enjoy writing erotic tales but that after his first bondage experience he had a genuine flair for it. Writing to erotic oriented magazines about his first bondage experience truly opened the floodgates for Christopher where this style of writing is concerned. Christopher thanks the handsome and muscular "Greg" for that experience way back in time. Christopher took "Creative Writing" courses every semester during his high school years and while other friends of his stopped writing what they loved to write about as time went on Christopher never let a day go by when he didn't write something... "I feel that if I don't write every day I will die," Christopher has said many times over.

Foot fetish stories and all things related; spanking fetish, erotic shaving, muscle bondage, tickle torture, and hardcore stories are just a few of the areas of gay eroticism that Christopher enjoys writing about and inspiring in others as well. As one internet buddy said to Christopher where the black socks fetish is concerned, "Until I started talking with you I never gave a thought to my socks when I got dressed for work in the morning. Now when I pull my dress socks on every morning I get a chill up my spine."

Christopher is proud of the erotic effect he has on people...

Christopher Trevor is also the author of:

> **The Executive Guide to Foot Fetishism and Office Discipline**
> 1-887895-36-1

> **Executive Ties That Bind**
> 1-887895-37-X

> **Don't!! Stop!! That Tickles!!**
> 1-887895-31-0

The Taming of Dominick
 1-887895-45-0

Timmy and The Hong Kong Tailor
 1-887895-30-2

Love, Torture and Redemption
 1-887895-32-9

Timmys Ticklish Trials
 978-1-887895-74-3

The Gym Instructor
 978-1-887895-44-6

Erotic Street Blues
 978-1-887895-97-2

Look for them where you found this book or Goodboner.com.

www.ingramcontent.com/pod-product-compliance
Lightning Source LLC
Chambersburg PA
CBHW070757280626
47162CB00016B/1375